In Search of Sam

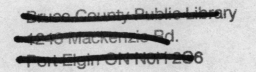

Also by Kristin Butcher

Truths I Learned from Sam
The Last Superhero

KRISTIN BUTCHER

In Search of Sam

DUNDURN
TORONTO

Editor: Allister Thompson
Design: Courtney Horner and Martin Gould
Printer: Webcom

Cover Design: Sarah Beaudin
Cover Image: Richard Aparicio

Library and Archives Canada Cataloguing in Publication

Butcher, Kristin, author
       In search of Sam / Kristin Butcher.

Issued in print and electronic formats.
ISBN 978-1-4597-2960-5 (pbk.).--ISBN 978-1-4597-2961-2
(pdf).--ISBN 978-1-4597-2962-9 (epub)

       I. Title.

PS8553.U6972I52 2015   jC813'.54   C2014-906766-6   C2014-906767-4

1 2 3 4 5   19 18 17 16 15

We acknowledge the support of the **Canada Council for the Arts** and the **Ontario Arts Council** for our publishing program. We also acknowledge the financial support of the **Government of Canada** through the **Canada Book Fund** and **Livres Canada Books**, and the **Government of Ontario** through the **Ontario Book Publishing Tax Credit** and the **Ontario Media Development Corporation.**

Care has been taken to trace the ownership of copyright material used in this book. The author and the publisher welcome any information enabling them to rectify any references or credits in subsequent editions.

J. Kirk Howard, President

The publisher is not responsible for websites or their content unless they are owned by the publisher.

Printed and bound in Canada.

VISIT US AT
Dundurn.com | @dundurnpress | Facebook.com/dundurnpress | Pinterest.com/dundurnpress

Dundurn
3 Church Street, Suite 500
Toronto, Ontario, Canada
M5E 1M2

For my mother one more time

Chapter One

SAM DIED ON NOVEMBER 11TH. Remembrance Day.
Like I could ever forget.

It's been four months already, but my feelings are
still raw, simmering just below the surface, ready to
bubble over all the time. The littlest things make me
cry — a baseball commercial, a cooking program, the
cowboy boots in my closet. Anything even remotely
related to Sam sets me off. *Anything*. It's dumb — I
know, but I can't help it. Sam was my father. I can't
just get over him. Mom says healing takes time, but
I have a feeling nothing less than a miracle is going
to get me past this.

I don't want to accept that Sam's gone. I still
think I'm going to see him again. If I hop on a bus for
Webb's River, he'll be waiting outside the motel at the
other end — tall and skinny, all blue jeans and cowboy

hat, his smile hiding behind that huge moustache, his piercing black eyes looking right through me. I hold the memory of him tight to my heart. Sam and I only had one summer together, but he changed my whole life.

I look down at the letter in my hand. *Dear Miss Lancaster.* I've already read it twice, but my brain is too fried to make sense of the words. Either that or legalese is a foreign language. The logo at the top is impressive, though — lots of scrollwork and gold lettering. *Morgan, Munson, and Bradley, Barristers and Solicitors.* Aren't barristers and solicitors the same thing? The letter is from Mr. R.A. Morgan. I wonder what the R and A stand for. Reginald Alfred? Rupert Angus? What about Rowland Ames? I run a few more lawyer-type names through my head, but I can't settle on anything I like so I abandon Mr. Morgan's name and turn my attention back to his letter.

This time it sinks in. I have to read around a bunch of *hereinafters, in as much ases, gift causa mortises,* and *remaindermans,* but I get the general idea. Bottom line — Sam left his estate to me, but there are papers to be signed before Mr. Morgan can turn it over. He doesn't say what it is I'm inheriting, but I assume it's Sam's trailer, truck, and land. If he had anything else, I don't know about it.

The only problem is the lawyer is in Kamloops and I'm in Vancouver. That means a road trip. I could take the bus or a plane, but then I'd have no transportation when I got there. Of course, I have no car either, but a vehicle has been on my wish list ever since I got my driver's license. The savings account my mom started when I was born and turned over to me on my last birthday could make that happen.

As for how long it will take to go and come back, that doesn't matter. I fast-tracked my way through high school and finished at the end of January, the day I turned eighteen. Two of life's milestones in one swoop. Anyway, until I start university next fall, my time is my own. I was going to look for a part-time job, but that can wait until after I meet with the lawyer. The only thing that might stand in my way is my mother.

"If we book an appointment with the lawyer, we can return the same day," she says when I tell her my plan. "There are lots of flights between Kamloops and Vancouver."

I shake my head. "You're not listening to me, Mom. This is something I want to do on my own. It's between Sam and me," I say.

She clucks her tongue and rolls her eyes. "Only you could romanticize something like this. We're talking lawyers, Dani. You are barely eighteen. You have no experience with something like this."

What she says is true, and I am a bit nervous about tackling it by myself, but I'm not about to admit that to her. "Sam had a will. All I have to do is sign some papers."

"And then what?"

"What do you mean?"

"After you sign the papers, then what will you do?"

I scowl. "I don't know. I guess it depends on what's in Sam's will."

"According to the letter from Mr. Morgan, Sam left you everything. That would be his property, his trailer, and all its contents."

"And Lizzie," I add.

Mom cocks her head quizzically.

"His truck," I explain.

She nods impatiently. "Whatever. What are you going to do with all these things?"

"Do I *have* to do something with them?"

"Are you saying you want to keep them?"

"I don't know. I can't decide that yet. I have to live with the idea a bit. What's the rush?"

Mom shuts her eyes. When she opens them again, they are shiny with unshed tears, and I am reminded that she loved Sam too. Though they never married and they split up before I was even born, I'm pretty sure part of her never got over him, and I know he never got over her. The only thing that came out of their relationship was me.

"Joanna, maybe Dani has a point," my stepdad, Reed, says. Until now, he's been sitting in the corner, saying nothing. "There really isn't a need to steamroll through this. Let Dani collect her inheritance and think on it for a while. What's the harm? We're talking land and a trailer."

My mother jumps right back into the fight. "And this nonsense about a car and driving to Kamloops?"

Reed licks his lips. "To tell you the truth, I think it's time Dani got a car. In the fall she'll be off to university and she can't always be relying on public transit."

Mom leaps out of her chair, waving her arms. "You think it's a good idea for her to drive across the province by herself?"

Reed holds up his hands. "That's not what I said."

"Well, that's what it sounded like."

"Just hear me out — okay? What if I help Dani choose a car? I'll make sure it's mechanically sound. Make sure it's not a lemon. Make sure she doesn't get ripped off. How would that be?"

My mother looks slightly mollified, but not completely. "I still don't want her driving to Kamloops alone. She's never driven outside Vancouver, for God's sake!"

Reed nods. "True. So what if I went with her?"

This time both Mom and I open our mouths to protest, but Reed shakes his head and continues talking, so we shut them again.

"I need to make a trip to the interior anyway. Remember, I said I wanted to set up a more central distribution centre for my brewery?"

I have no clue what he's talking about, but Mom nods.

"Well, there are a couple of locations on the way to Kamloops that I need to take a look at. We can kill two birds with one stone. I can take care of my business, and Dani can have company on her drive." He smiles at me. "Will that work for you, Dani?"

I nod. In a way I'm sort of relieved. The idea of driving all that way by myself was a little intimidating.

Reed turns to Mom. "And what about you?"

She frowns. "How long will you be gone?"

"Not more than a couple of days. I'll fly home."

Mom looks alarmed. "And what about Dani? How's she going to get back?"

"Drive?" I offer sarcastically.

Mom's mouth thins into a hard line. "I don't want you driving alone. It's only March. There could be snow."

Reed sighs. "Okay. So how about when Dani is finished everything she needs to do, one of us flies to Kamloops and drives back with her? We can play it by ear."

Mom shakes her head and scowls. "I don't like it."

"Mother," I protest, "I'm not a child, you know. In fact, I don't even need your permission to do this. I'm eighteen — an adult."

Reed sits back in his chair. His lips tremble as he tries to hide a smile. "She's got you there, Joanna."

———

Reed takes me vehicle shopping the very next day, and at the second car lot I fall in love with a little silver Honda Civic. It's about eight years old but there's not a scratch on it. So we get it checked out by a mechanic. Once it gets the okay from him, Reed and the car dealer start doing the *let's-make-a-deal* dance. I am totally fascinated listening to them dicker over the price and what it should include. Finally, they settle on a number, I sign a bunch of papers and hand over a huge chunk of my bank account, and *voilà*: I am a car owner.

Next on the agenda, I make an appointment to see the lawyer, and two days after that Reed and I are on the road. I'm so excited, I don't even mind getting up while it's still dark. Instead of travelling the Coquihalla Highway, which is the most direct way to get to Kamloops, we take the southerly route through Hope and Princeton into the Okanagan Valley, because that's the area Reed needs to check out.

Even at seven in the morning, there are a ton of cars on the highway, so to placate Mom, Reed navigates the Civic out of the city. Then I take over. It feels great to be driving my own vehicle. At Princeton we stop for a late breakfast, and then Reed takes the wheel again.

The locations he's interested in are tiny towns between Princeton and Kelowna.

"I would've thought you'd be looking to put your distribution centre in a big city," I say.

"It needs to be near a city, but out of the way is actually more convenient, as long as there's easy access to a major highway. That way I have a better chance of getting the space I need at a price I'm willing to pay. It means less congestion too. Mostly the brewery relies on big trucks, and semi-drivers aren't fond of manoeuvring through city streets. They prefer wide-open spaces."

"So did you see anything that'll work?"

He shrugs. "Nothing that blew my socks off. But I'm not in a rush. I'll keep looking."

It's suppertime when we finally get to Kamloops and pull into the parking lot of the hotel Mom booked for us. It's in the centre of downtown, and judging from the polished wood, sparkling chandeliers, and massive floral arrangements, it's pretty high-end. If it was up to me, I would have found an inexpensive motel, which — when I stop to think about it — is probably why Mom booked us into this place. It's her way of keeping me safe and under her wing. She also volunteered to pay for it, so who am I to argue?

Reed and I eat in the hotel dining room, complete with white linen, crystal, and gleaming silver. All I want is a hamburger, but that isn't even on the menu so I have seared halibut instead.

And that's when I run out of gas. Instead of recharging my batteries, dinner wipes me out completely. I can barely keep my eyes open through dessert.

"Go to bed," Reed laughs. "You've had a long day."

"Are you going to your room too?"

"In a while. My flight to Vancouver doesn't leave until noon tomorrow, and there's a lot of evening left. I think I'll go to the bar for a nightcap and call your mother to let her know we arrived safely."

"Okay," I say. "Tell her hi for me. See you in the morning." Then I give him a peck on the cheek and stumble off to my room.

Chapter Two

I'M EXCITED ABOUT BEING in Kamloops on my own
— until about three seconds after Reed's plane takes
off. That's when the sense of adventure evaporates
and all my mother's arguments against the trip flood
my brain. My stomach becomes a queasy knot Harry
Houdini couldn't have untied, and without warning
my knees give out. Thankfully, there's a bench behind
me, and I drop onto it like a sack of rocks.

An elderly man standing a few feet away glares
in my direction. I want to tell him my baby elephant
impersonation wasn't intentional but I know he
won't believe me, so even though it's too late to be
anonymous, I bow my head and hide behind the
curtain of my hair. Then I shut my eyes and give myself
a stern talking-to. Okay, so I'm alone in a strange
city. I don't know anyone and I don't know my way

around. That's okay. I have a car, money, cellphone, hotel room, and an appointment with a lawyer.

I glance at my watch. *Holy crap!* My meeting with Mr. Morgan is in fifty-five minutes, and though I have his address, I have no clue how to get there or where to park when I do.

Panic threatens to swamp me, but I squelch it with logic. My car has a GPS. All I have to do is plug in the address and go where it tells me.

I take a few deep breaths, stand up, and push my mother's voice to the back of my mind. Then I grab my backpack, sling it over my shoulder, and head for my car.

———

The firm of Morgan, Munson, and Bradley is in a suburban shopping mall, which I locate without a problem. I even arrive with time to spare. I park at the back of the lot, away from runaway shopping carts and other cars. My little Honda may not be new, but it's new to me, and I don't want any dings in it.

The glass door to the law office looks like it should belong to a drugstore (I was sort of expecting polished mahogany) and as I push it open, I imagine the lawyers on the other side dispensing legal advice like prescriptions. *Find two expert witnesses and call me in the morning.* But to my surprise the office is actually very lawyerish and lavish, all plush carpet and wingback leather chairs.

The receptionist fits in perfectly. In fact, she

could've come directly from the *Forbes* magazine lying on the lacquered coffee table. Her makeup is flawless, there's not a single hair out of place, her lipstick is intact, and her designer suit couldn't crease if it tried. When I present myself to her, she doesn't smile. I'm guessing that might crack the makeup.

"Please have a seat." She nods toward the collection of leather chairs. "Mr. Morgan will be with you shortly."

She got that right. Two seconds after I sit down, a wiry little guy wearing brown dress pants and a white dress shirt with rolled-up sleeves comes striding towards me. He must have had a tough morning because his tie is loosened and the top button of his shirt is undone. He looks to be in his mid-thirties. He's not balding, but his straight blond hair is sparse, cut short except for a forelock that keeps sliding into his eyes. In the time it takes him to cross the room he brushes it back three times. His skin is pale and pockmarked. Teenage acne victim, probably. His blue eyes, watered down so much they're almost colourless, practically disappear behind black-rimmed glasses. He smiles, baring crooked teeth.

But there's an energy and friendliness about him that draws me in, and my anxiety starts to melt away. Unlike the receptionist, there are no airs about this man. I can see why Sam chose him for his lawyer.

"Bob Morgan." He stretches out a hand. For a small guy, he has a firm handshake — but cold, as if he'd been making snowballs.

"Dani Lancaster," I say. "I'm Sam Swan's daughter."

He nods. "Yes. I'm sorry. Your dad was one of the good guys."

I'm not ready for that, and uninvited tears spring to my eyes. I try to blink them away.

I know Bob Morgan notices, but he doesn't comment. Instead he extends an arm toward the hallway. "Shall we go to my office?"

By the time I take the chair he offers me, I have my emotions back under control, but considering why I'm here, it's going to be almost impossible to banish Sam from my thoughts. I try to focus on the folder Bob Morgan is opening. It's not very thick, and it pains me to realize that's all that's left of Sam's life. I feel my throat tighten. *Damn it!* I can't let myself think about him.

Bob Morgan cuts into my thoughts. "Your father made sure all his affairs were in order. He didn't want to leave any loose ends. With the exception of his horse, which he bequeathed to the Tooby family at Greener Pastures Ranch, he left his entire estate to you. He wanted you to know that he would have left you the horse too, but it wasn't practical. However, I have been in touch with the Toobys, and they said to tell you that you are welcome to ride her anytime."

I bite my bottom lip to keep it from trembling. "Thank you." I can barely get the words out.

He offers me an encouraging smile. "This shouldn't take too long," he says. "It's all pretty straightforward, exactly as I explained in my letter. I just need you to sign some papers."

I sit forward in my chair and take the pen he offers. He explains each document before I sign, but my brain won't let the words in. I don't even remember writing my name, but I must have, because as I gaze down at the papers in front of me, there it is.

Bob Morgan is talking again, so I force myself to listen. "In addition to the acreage, trailer, and vehicle, your father left you some money." He reaches into the folder again and passes me a white envelope. I just stare at it, so he says, "It's a cheque — not a fortune but still a tidy sum. Sam didn't specify how it was to be used — that's up to you — but he thought it was sufficient to cover the cost of a university education. I suggest you deposit it in your bank account as soon as you can. You don't want to be walking around with that kind of money in your pocket."

He opens the drawer again, pulls out a manila envelope, and passes it to me. "A few other documents you may need," he says. Then he sets a keyring on the desk in front of me.

I gaze blankly at it for several seconds. Sam's keys. My keys now. My throat tightens again. I pick up the ring and wrap my fingers around the keys one at a time. The trailer. The shed. Lizzie. But I don't recognize the last key. I hold it up and frown.

"Safety deposit box," Bob Morgan explains. He flips through the papers in the folder. "The bank is right in this mall. Just present the key, your ID, and Sam's death certificate — that's in the manila envelope — and the bank will provide you with access. There's a letter from this office in the envelope as well, verifying that the will has been settled and you are the heir."

He sits back in his chair with a sigh. "And that about does it. Will you be going to Webb's River?"

I fiddle with the keys. "I guess so. Maybe." I look numbly across at the lawyer. "I don't know. Suddenly I feel a little shell-shocked. I need some time to think."

He nods and smiles. "Of course you do. This is a lot to take in. Is someone here with you?"

I shake my head. "My stepdad drove up with me, but he had to fly back to Vancouver, so now I'm by myself."

Bob Morgan looks surprised.

"My choice," I add quickly. "My mom wanted to be here too, but I said I had to do this on my own." I shrug. "I don't know. Maybe I should have let her come."

He walks around his desk and perches on the corner. Then he smiles. "You don't have to make any decisions today, Dani. Put the cheque in the bank and empty the safety deposit box. After that, just take it slow. In a few weeks or months, you'll get sorted, and then you can decide how you want to handle things. You don't have to rush."

I smile gratefully. "That's what my stepdad says too."

"Smart man. Listen to him." He stands up, so I do too. He looks solemnly into my eyes. "And if you have any questions or need any help with anything — anything at all — you have my number. Just pick up the phone."

———

When I exit Morgan, Munson, and Bradley, my head is spinning, and I wander through the mall like a robot. I couldn't be more out in space if I were on drugs. Eventually I end up in the food court and sink onto a stool at one of the tables.

It's the aroma of frying onions that finally penetrates the fog in my head. My stomach growls. "Right," I mumble under my breath. Maybe food will help me think straight.

By the time I finish my sub and iced tea, I know what I'm going to do — at least for the next half hour.

I go in search of the bank. Apparently I passed it during my brain-dead stroll through the mall, but I have zero memory of it. I have an account with that bank so before I see a teller about Sam's safety deposit box, I stop at the ATM to deposit the cheque Bob Morgan gave me.

Whoa! I do a double take when I pull it out of the envelope. It's for $75,000. That's a lot of money. It makes me nervous even holding the cheque. I endorse it and deposit it as fast as I can. When the machine spits out my receipt, I glance around nervously and tuck it into a hidden compartment of my wallet.

Inside the bank, there's a long lineup, and it's a good ten minutes before I reach a teller — for all the good it does me. She sends me somewhere else, where it takes ten minutes more to verify I am who I say I am. Even though I have the letter from Bob Morgan, the safety deposit box key, and Sam's death certificate, the bank employee calls the law office to make sure I'm not trying to pull a fast one.

Finally I'm taken to a small room lined with metal boxes. It reminds me of a post office. The bank person uses her key, I use mine, and suddenly I'm alone in this fluorescent cell with a long, skinny box.

I lift the lid. Inside is a white plastic grocery bag. I smile. It is so Sam. As I lift it out, I can tell from the feel that it contains more papers, but also some objects. I'm curious to find out exactly what, but my brain is already on overload. If I try to shove in any more information, I'll either blow a fuse or melt. So I stuff the bag into my backpack with the manila envelope. Then I let myself out of the room, relinquish the key — I won't be using the safety deposit box again — and exit the mall.

Back in my hotel room, I sit cross-legged on the bed and dump my backpack. I glance from the manila envelope to the grocery bag and back again. Where should I start? The envelope is all about the red tape of dying. But the grocery bag is Sam.

As I pick it up, I imagine him placing things inside, so I'm teary before I even open it.

I spill the contents onto the bed. There are several items, but I see only one: a letter addressed to me. *For my daughter.*

Now I'm really crying. How can my heart hurt so much?

Carefully — I don't want to destroy even the envelope — I open it. As I unfold the paper, Sam's handwriting jumps off the page. It's as if he's right there in the room with me. Through blurred eyes, I start to read.

Dear Dani ...

Chapter Three

... *I'm not sure why I'm writing this except to hang on. Hang on to what's real. Hang on to you. I hope you'll hang on to me too. I know that's a selfish thing to ask, especially considering the short time we've shared and the circumstances that brought us together, but that doesn't stop me from hoping you'll think of me from time to time. Before I got cancer, my life was good. I was happy. But then you came to Webb's River and filled a mighty hole I hadn't even known was there. When you found out who I was, you could have hated me. You had every right. But you didn't. That brings me more comfort than you can know, and because of that I am at peace when I contemplate what lies ahead.*

If you're reading this letter, you already have your inheritance. No strings attached. You know better than me what you should do with it.

I think this is the part where I'm supposed to pass along some wise, fatherly advice. There are a couple of problems with that. First of all, I was never really a father to you and second of all, I'm a long way from wise. If you could learn from my mistakes, it would be a different story. I'd have a ton to teach you. But that's not how it works. We all live our own lives and make our own mistakes. If we're lucky, we don't do too much damage along the way — to ourselves or anybody else. I've always met life head on, and I have no regrets. A person can't ask for more than that.

Your mom has done a great job raising you. You're a heck of a kid. Just listen to your heart (and your mother) and you'll do just fine.

Love,

Sam

I lower the letter, clap a hand over my mouth, and rock backward and forward. The room is a blur. I can't breathe. I try to choke back a sob, but I can't do that either. The muscles in my throat have locked so the sob stays lodged like a rock right where it is. Fat tears spill from my eyes and splatter onto the paper. I brush them away with my sleeve; I don't want Sam's last words to be washed away. They're all I have left.

I use my sleeve on my eyes now and push myself off the bed. In the bathroom I blow my nose and splash cold water on my face. I look at myself in the mirror. Already my skin is blotchy and my nose is red. Sam told me I'm not very pretty when I cry. He was right.

I sob and laugh at the same time, and then hiccup as the two collide.

I breathe deeply, straighten my shoulders, and glare sternly at my image. I can't keep falling to pieces. It won't bring Sam back. Silent reprimand over, I march back into the other room and climb onto the bed again.

I carefully refold Sam's letter. I know I'll read it a thousand times more, but right now I have to wade through the rest of his papers and belongings. I reach for the manila envelope in the hope that poking through boring legal documents will give my emotions a chance to level out.

It does. I never thought I could be interested in deeds, vehicle and property insurance, or tax returns, but I pore over them like there's going to be a test after, and then it hits me: this information matters. Sam's land, his truck, his trailer — they're all mine now, and I need to understand what owning them involves. I can't just wander through fields of flowers any more; I have to pay taxes on them!

Until this moment I hadn't realized what it meant to inherit these things. Somewhere in the back of my mind I just sort of thought I could keep Sam's land and possessions in my memory along with him, because they belong together, but that's not how it is. I can't visit Sam's trailer on a whim now and again and expect it to stay the same. Sam may live in my memory, but his property and belongings are very real, and I have to deal with them. I don't have to make any decisions about them yet, but I need to understand what my responsibilities are if I decide to keep them. It's hard to get my head around that. Last month I was a kid in high school, and my biggest concern was getting homework done. Now suddenly I have to start thinking like an adult.

That's when I realize I have to go to Webb's River. Before I can change my mind, I grab my phone and call my mother. I tell her about the lawyer's office and the safety deposit box. I assure her that everything is in order and that I am reading through Sam's papers. I don't mention the money Sam left me. That will only set her off on a tangent, and I can't deal with that right now. I tell her I'm fine, ask if Reed got back to Vancouver safely, and then, before she can volunteer to fly up to Kamloops to drive me home, I tell her I'm going to Webb's River. She's not pleased and tries to talk me out of going, but I stand my ground. I say I'm driving to Sam's place first thing in the morning. I may stay just for the day or I may overnight it, depending on what I find. Then, promising to call again tomorrow night, I give her my love and hang up.

I stare at the phone a good two minutes, waiting for my mother to call back. But she doesn't so I set the phone on the table beside the bed and stuff the legal papers back into the manila envelope. All that's left on the bed are the personal items from the plastic grocery bag.

I start with the obvious: Sam's wallet. Like his hat, his jeans, his boots, even the laugh lines on his face, the wallet has been moulded to fit him. It is curved from sitting in his back pocket, conforming to the saddle and the seat of his truck. The tan-coloured leather is shiny smooth, except at the edges, where the finish has been rubbed completely away, and along the fold, which is a web of cracked lines.

At first all I do is turn the wallet over in my hands. I can't bring myself to open it. I don't want to invade Sam's privacy. But then I remind myself that he left it to me. He expects — expected — me to go through it.

There's not much in it — not even money — just a driver's license and social insurance card. The other slots are empty. There are no slips of paper with phone numbers, no ticket stubs, no business cards, no dry cleaning receipts, none of the usual bits and pieces people accumulate in their wallets, and it occurs to me that Sam may have cleaned out his billfold before he died. Then I remember his trailer, truck, and shed. There were no extras there either. Sam was as uncomplicated as a person can be.

And just as private.

I poke into every corner and crevice of the wallet, hoping for something, anything that will tell me more about this man who was my father. Sam was a foundling, so I know I won't find a birth certificate, but surely there is something to hint at his identity.

The compartment for bills has a lining, so I pry it up. I'm not really expecting to find anything underneath, but to my surprise, I do: a photograph of a little boy with dark, curly hair and sparkling black eyes. I flip it over. *Sam, age 4* it says on the back in shaky handwriting. Sam told me that as a baby he'd been left on the doorstep of an elderly couple, who, because they were afraid Sam would be taken from them, kept his existence hidden from the authorities. But when it was time for Sam to start school, they couldn't keep him a secret any longer, and just as they had feared, Sam was placed in foster care. He never saw the old couple again, so this picture might be the only thing he had to remind him of his first six years of life. I study it a while longer and then set it on the bed beside me.

I shift my position, and what looks like a necklace slides across the comforter and disappears under my knee. I fish it out and hold it up. It's a pendant on a silver chain. It seems an odd piece of jewellery for a man to have, so I examine it more closely. The chain is a good quality silver rope. The half-heart pendant is also silver. The thing is, it's been cut. I can tell by the rough, jagged inside edge. The other edges are smooth and rounded. My guess is it was once a whole heart, but for some reason half of it was cut away. The question is why?

Then I remember that Mom and Sam had identical turquoise gemstones. Could this half-heart be another love token they shared? Does Mom have the other half of the heart? I make a mental note to ask her next time we talk, but I'm pretty sure I already know the answer. I'm as familiar with my mother's jewellery as she is. If she had half a silver heart lying around somewhere, I'd have seen it. I flip the pendant over, looking for an inscription. There isn't one. Nothing on the chain either.

So much for that. Unless Mom can tell me more or there's a clue mixed in with Sam's other belongings, the chain and pendant are a dead end.

I sigh and move on to a dog-eared envelope addressed to Sam. It's old. I can tell without even opening it. Not only is the envelope practically falling apart, it has a thirty-nine-cent stamp on it! There's a return address in the top left-hand corner: Mr. & Mrs. D. Sheffield, 422 Owen Way, Merritt, B.C. Neither the name nor address rings any bells.

Curious, I slip the letter from the envelope. My gaze goes immediately to the date at the top of the page: July 12, 1991. That's over twenty years ago. Quickly I scan the letter. It's from one of Sam's foster families. Probably his last one, if the date is any indication. In 1991 Sam would've been nineteen, and I know he joined the rodeo shortly after he graduated high school.

The letter is full of news about life in the Sheffield home and asks how Sam is doing too. Obviously these people cared about him. Why else would they write to him after he left? Besides, they ask when he'll be back for a visit, and they sign off with love. Sam never talked about the families he lived with, but this one must have been special if he hung on to the letter. As I return it to its envelope, I can't help wondering if Sam wrote back and if he ever went to see them.

The last item on the bed is an address book. If there are going to be any clues to Sam's identity, this is where I'll find them. With high hopes, I flip through it. It's disappointingly empty. I shouldn't be surprised, but I am. It contains Mom's address and phone number, of course — scratched out and re-entered after each of her five marriages, but otherwise it's just a collection of business numbers: doctor, drugstore, lawyer, rodeo association, farrier, feed store, that sort of thing.

There is one entry that catches my attention, though. It's for an Arlo — no last name. Nellie Hill's Boarding House, Kamloops, is scribbled on the address line. And there's a phone number. Unless Arlo was Sam's dentist or barber, this could be a lead.

Chapter Four

IT'S DARK WHEN I HEAD OUT the next morning, and since I have no idea which way to go, even in daylight, I have to trust the GPS to guide me. In just a few turns I'm on Highway 97, and I relax my steel grip on the steering wheel. I still don't know where I'm going, but I do know Highway 97 runs through Webb's River, so I'm pretty sure I can't get lost. According to the GPS, it's a two-hour drive.

Dull grey light gradually pushes away the darkness, revealing scraps of snow among the trees and scraggly clumps of winter grass at the side of the road — a detail I won't share with my mother. At least not until I'm back in Vancouver. Even though the snow is several days old and the highway is totally clear, the mere existence of the white stuff will have her on the next plane to Kamloops.

As the morning wears on, I search the sky for the sun, but it stays resolutely hidden behind dirty clouds, and I find myself being dragged down by the bleakness of the day. The closer I get to Webb's River, the more uneasy I become.

It's not that I question whether or not I should be going. I know I should be. I *have to* — for practical reasons as well as personal ones. For one thing, I need to make sure there's no business stuff that's been overlooked. I'm fairly certain there isn't; Sam was pretty thorough, but you never know. If Mom was with me, I wouldn't be nearly so anxious, but that's because she would be running the show. And it can't be that way. All Sam and I had were six short weeks together, and almost all of that was spent at his place in Webb's River. If it hurts to think about him when I'm in Vancouver, it's going to be a hundred times worse at his trailer. But I have to do it.

I'm so busy rationalizing all this in my head that I stop seeing my surroundings, and the next thing I know, I've arrived. The sign is right there: *Webb's River: population 1,123*. Next up is the road leading to Greener Pastures Ranch, and my heart skips a few beats. I spent as much time there last summer as I did at Sam's place. It started when Sam signed me up for riding lessons, but somewhere along the way my instructor became my boyfriend. But that's over now. Micah and I both hoped our relationship would be more than a summer romance, but with him at university in Calgary and me in Vancouver, it wasn't working. We still exchange texts and emails, but as friends.

A little farther up the highway, I flick on my turn signal, slow down, and steer my little Honda onto the road leading to Sam's place. I know the trailer and property are mine now, but in my heart they will always belong to Sam.

As happens so often these days when I think about him, emotions threaten to swamp me, so I open the window and allow a blast of cold air to shock them away. The farther I get from the highway, the more leftover snow there is, and I am forced to concentrate on my driving. But as soon as I round the final stand of fir trees and see the trailer, my head is once more filled with Sam.

The Honda crunches to a stop near the fire pit, and I turn off the engine. The world is so quiet, I imagine this is what it must feel like to be deaf. I reach into my pocket for Sam's keys and, clutching them so tightly they dig into my palm, I stare hard at the trailer. Now that I'm here, I don't want to go in. It's not summer anymore. There won't be wonderful smells coming from the kitchen, no wildflowers on the table, and no baseball game blaring from the television. The trailer will be cold and quiet and empty. It will mean Sam really is gone.

I get out of the car. It's windy, so I zip up my jacket, shove my hands into my pockets, and pick my way around the piles of snow to the shed.

Sam always kept the doors open, so it feels wrong to see them shut tight. I find the appropriate key and remove the padlock. Inside it's dark and damp and smells of wet hay. I hear a horse whinny, but that's impossible. Jasmine has been gone for months. The fence separating her stall from the rest of the shed is gone too. The shed isn't empty, though. In fact, it's as full as it can be — full of Lizzie.

I run my hand over the truck's faded red fender to the driver's door. Fishing the keys out of my pocket again, I open it and climb inside. The cold vinyl of the seat crackles as I slide behind the wheel. I pat the dash.

"How're you doing, Lizzie?"

I stick the key into the ignition and without even thinking put one foot on the brake and the other on the clutch. Instantly I'm taken back to the afternoon Sam taught me to drive Lizzie. I can't help smiling. I'd never operated a standard transmission before, and I bucked poor Lizzie — and Sam — all over the field.

I turn the key. Nothing. I don't bother trying it again. Common sense says Sam took the battery out, but my heart says Lizzie's in mourning.

"I miss him too," I say, patting the dash again and letting myself out of the truck.

I lock the shed, sigh, and head for the trailer. No point putting off the inevitable any longer. I remind myself what I'm here to do: keep my eyes peeled for business documents, collect the photographs from the living room cabinet, find the string tie with the turquoise gemstone, and round up any other personal items Sam may have left. If I keep my mind on those tasks, I'll be fine.

As I step inside I'm met by a musty odour, but otherwise the trailer is the same — the toilet seat in the bathroom is even up — and for a second I imagine that Sam has stepped out for a cigarette or gone for a ride on Jasmine. There are still books piled on the living room floor and crammed on the shelves in the reading room. A thick novel lies face down on the futon. Was this the last book Sam read? I pick it up and smile at the title. Espionage novels were Sam's favourite. I place the book in the box with the photographs. Then I carry on to the kitchen. It's even more bare bones than I remember. Did Sam and I really create gourmet meals here? My gaze wanders to the fridge, open, empty, and unplugged, and the happy memory evaporates. That was then and this is now. I poke through the cupboards and drawers, but there is nothing that screams Sam.

I cup my hands and blow on them. It's almost as cold in the trailer as it is outside. I stare toward the end of the hall and frown. Just one more space to check out: Sam's bedroom. I was only ever in it once, the day I discovered Sam was dying. I never went in it again after that and I still don't want to, but it's the only place there might be pieces of Sam I don't know about.

Before I can change my mind, I hurry down the length of the trailer and through the open doorway. I feel Sam here more than anywhere else, so I avoid opening myself to the room. Instead I focus on examining its parts. The drawer of the bedside table contains a blank notepad and some rodeo magazines. A box on the floor is heaped with belts and old boots. A zippered bag slung on a hanger is stuffed with mismatched socks. That makes me smile. Sam must have been waiting for the mates to show up. I actually have to hunt for the string tie, but I eventually find it draped over a nail at the back of the closet. The triangular-shaped turquoise is cold and smooth, and as I clutch it fiercely, I see Sam at the potluck supper as clearly as if he were standing in front of me this very second. My body goes weak and I sink onto the bed. Tears roll down my cheeks.

"Oh, Sam." The words catch in my throat. The tears come faster, and soon I'm crying so hard I can't breathe. I don't care. I topple sideways and bury my face in Sam's pillow, giving myself up to grief. Finally my lungs scream for air, and as I gasp it in, my senses reel with his scent.

My tears are shocked away. Pushing myself back to a sitting position, I tug the pillow free of the bed cover and hug it close, breathing Sam in until I feel lightheaded. I can't get enough of his smell. It's so real, so tangible. It's like he left a part of himself here on purpose to help me through this ordeal.

I don't know how long I sit there, but eventually I add the string tie and pillow to the box and let myself out of the trailer.

When I get to the car, fine snow has started to fall. I stow the box of meagre treasures in the Honda's trunk and take my place behind the wheel. Suddenly it's like somebody pulled my plug, and as the tension drains from my body, I close my eyes and collapse against the seat.

My stomach growls, hauling me back to reality. The snow is coming down faster now. Time to return to Kamloops. As I steer the car toward the road leading to the highway, I look at Sam's place one last time through the rear-view mirror. Maybe Mom's right. Maybe all I need to heal is time. Maybe it'll be easier in the summer. Then I round the stand of fir trees and Sam's place disappears from sight. But it doesn't matter. In my mind, I'm already coming back.

Chapter Five

THE SNOW STOPS AS I TURN onto Highway 97, and with that last bit of stress out of the way, I feel more relaxed than I have since I left Vancouver. It isn't just because I don't have to white-knuckle it back to Kamloops, and it isn't because I'm distancing myself from Webb's River and memories of Sam. It's more like I'm coming to terms with those memories. Crazy as it sounds, it's like Sam and I are patching up an argument. Things aren't back to the way they were before — they never can be, but I can start moving on. I've faced my ghosts. I've met them head on and recognized them for what they are: memories. It's my choice whether they bring me joy or pain.

Mentally I tick off the tasks on my to-do list. I've dealt with the lawyer and the bank. I've checked out the trailer, the shed, and Lizzie. I've looked through

Sam's legal papers and the bag of personal items he left in his safety deposit box. And I did it all in just a day and a half.

I smile and give the steering wheel a congratulatory pat. Then I become sombre again. Does this mean it's time to head home? I immediately dismiss the idea. I'm not ready. I've only just begun to stretch my wings. Besides, I feel like I still have unfinished business.

That's when I remember Sam's address book and the entry for someone named Arlo at a boarding house in Kamloops. I want to believe this Arlo person knows something that will open a door to Sam's past. I shouldn't get my hopes up, but if I don't at least check the guy out, I know I'll kick myself later.

It's mid-afternoon by the time I get back to Kamloops, and I'm starved, so I pick up a burger on the way to the hotel and eat it as I go through Sam's personal stuff again. It doesn't tell me anything more than it did before. And yet I know these things have to mean something, or Sam wouldn't have kept them.

Swallowing the last of my burger, I flip through the address book to the Arlo entry and punch the number for the boarding house into my phone. Someone picks up after the very first ring.

"Hello." I can barely hear the woman on the other end over the rock music blaring in the background. "Kerry, turn that blasted radio down! I'm on the phone." Almost immediately, the music stops and the woman says, "Sorry 'bout that. Dang kids and their music. They're going to make us all deaf."

I don't tell the woman I'm probably around the same age as the girl she was bellowing at. Instead I clear my throat and try to sound mature. "Is this Nellie's Boarding House?"

"Sure is, sugar, but there ain't no vacancies right now. Sorry. You might wanna try Grifton House. I think it's got a room to let. The number's in the book."

I can tell the woman is about to hang up, so I quickly say, "Actually, I'm not looking for a room. I'm looking for information."

The woman is suddenly wary. "Oh, yeah? What kind of information?"

There's no short answer to that. I clear my throat again to buy some think time. "My name is Dani Lancaster," I begin, "and I'm trying to locate a man named Arlo. Sorry, I don't have a last name, just this phone number." When the woman doesn't answer, I add, "He was a friend of my father, Sam Swan."

I don't know why, but that does the trick.

"You're Sam Swan's daughter?" The woman sounds incredulous. "I didn't know Sammy had any kids."

It would take an age to explain the relationship between Sam and me. Besides, it's none of this woman's business. So I just say, "I live with my mother."

"Hmmph. I never woulda taken Sammy for a family man. So how is he, anyway? I can't remember the last time I saw him."

"He passed away," I say quietly. "Last November."

"Sammy's dead? No! You're joshing me."

Her voice is loud and grating. I pull away from the phone and wince before replying. "No. It's true." Then, because I know she'll ask, I say, "He had cancer. I'm here in Kamloops to settle his will. I found this number in his address book."

"What did you say your name was?"

"Dani Lancaster."

"Lancaster, huh? Is that your mother's name?"

This is one nosy lady. I don't have anything to hide but nevertheless I sidestep the question. "Mrs. — er, Nellie, would Arlo be there, by any chance?"

Her laugh is like a witch's cackle. "God, no. Arlo moved out a couple of years back. I woulda thought you'd know that, seein' as how it was Sam what set him up in that trailer."

At first I'm confused, but then I realize Nellie isn't referring to Sam's trailer. I'm disappointed and hopeful at the same time. "In Kamloops? Do you have an address?"

"No, not here. It's in Barriere. Sam got a good deal on some land there after the big fire a few years back. At least that's what Arlo said. Anyway, that's where he is. Unless he's moved again. I wouldn't know about that."

"Did he leave a forwarding address or a phone number?"

"I ain't his keeper, sugar. All I know is he lives in a trailer in Barriere."

I can tell she's getting ready to hang up again. "Just one more thing," I say before that happens. "Could you tell me Arlo's last name?"

She cackles again. "Jones, if you can believe it."

Then there's a click and the line goes dead. Goodbye Nellie's Boarding House. Hello Internet white pages. I shift gears without even blinking. How did people function before smart phones? I type in Arlo's full name and Barriere, B.C., then cross my fingers and wait. *Jones* is such a common surname, I could end up with fifty hits. On the other hand, Arlo is pretty uncommon, so that should narrow things down.

The results come up in a matter of seconds. There are no listings for Arlo Jones, but there are several for A. Jones. One in McLure, a couple more in Kamloops, and one in Barriere.

Bingo!

I quickly punch the number into my phone. After three rings, I glance at my watch. Four o'clock. Arlo could still be at work. By the fifth ring, I'm ready to hang up. And then someone picks up.

"Hello," says a man.

"Hello," I reply. "My name is Dani Lan —"

He cuts me off before I can finish. "What are you selling?"

That catches me by surprise. "Excuse me?"

"Call display says you're an unknown number, which means you're probably selling something. What?"

"I'm not selling anything," I assure him. The next words gush from my mouth before he can hang up. "My name is Dani Lancaster. I'm Sam Swan's daughter, and I'm looking for someone named Arlo Jones."

He doesn't answer.

"Are you still there?"

"Sam doesn't have a daughter. What are you trying to pull here? If you think you can scam me out of some money, you're tough out of luck. I don't have any."

"I'm not selling anything," I insist. "Really. I swear." Even though he can't see me, I cross my heart. My fingers too. What I thought was going to be a simple phone call is turning out to be more like a war. Why does everyone want to hang up on me? Panicking, I blurt, "Sam is dead. And yes, he does have a daughter. Me. One of the things he left me was his address book, and your name was in it. I called Nellie's Boarding House, and she said you'd moved to Barriere." I take a breath before continuing. "I only found out Sam was my father last summer, so we didn't have much time to get to know each other." I pause and then add nervously, "I was hoping you might be able to tell me about him."

Another long pause. Finally Arlo says, "Sam is dead? I didn't know. I can't believe it. How? When? Was it an accident?" I can hear the shock and disbelief in his voice, and my own grief returns.

I bite the inside of my lip hard, willing physical pain to chase away the emotional one. "Cancer," I say. "Last November." I want to tell him it was quick. But it wasn't. I want to say Sam didn't suffer. But he did.

"I can't believe it," Arlo says again. "I just can't believe it."

Again the line goes quiet. "I'm sorry," I say. My voice is shaking. "I know it's a shock."

"Yeah. It's that all right." Arlo sounds shaky too. "Sam was a good man — and a good friend. I can't think when I saw him last, but then Sam was never one to keep in touch. It's hard when you're in rodeo. You're on the road so much. It's been a while, but I remember."

"Were you in rodeo too?" I need to get the conversation on safer ground.

"Over ten years. Still would be if I hadn't had that accident. But that's not important now." He pushes on. "You say you want to find out about your dad. I'm not sure how much I can tell you, but we could meet for a coffee and talk if you like. Where are you?"

"Kamloops."

"That's a bit of a haul, and I don't have a car," he says.

"I do," I tell him, suddenly hopeful. "I can come to Barriere. We can meet wherever you like."

To my surprise, he laughs. "No grass growing under your feet, is there?"

I'm glad he can't see me blush. "Too anxious?"

"No. To tell you the truth, straightforward is a nice change. As it turns out, tomorrow is my day off, so if you want to drive up then, we could meet for coffee. There's a little restaurant on Highway 5 as you come into town. You can't miss it. It's about an hour's drive. Does ten o'clock work for you?"

"Ten o'clock is great."

"Okay, we'll see you tomorrow. Bye now."

"Bye, Arlo. And thanks."

When I switch off the phone I'm smiling so hard, my cheeks hurt. *Yes!* I'm finally going to learn something about Sam. I retrieve the complimentary hotel notepad and pen from the desk and start to scribble down questions. *How did you and Sam meet? How long were you friends? What other friends did he have? Did he ever mention people from his past? Did Sam say where he grew up? Was Sam ever in a relationship? When did —*

The questions are coming fast and furious when my phone rings and interrupts my momentum. I glance at the display screen. It's my mother. I cast my gaze towards the ceiling and put down the pen. No point ignoring her. She'll just keep calling.

"Hey, Mom." I use my cheeriest voice. "How's it going?"

"Fine. How's it going with you? Did you go to Webb's River?"

"Uh-huh. I got back about an hour ago."

"And?"

"And what?"

She clucks her tongue in annoyance. "What do you think? How was everything?"

There's no sense lying. She knows me too well. "Everything was locked up, but nothing was too different. There were lots of memories for sure. I got misty a couple of times. But I'm okay. I'm glad I went. I think it gave me some closure."

"That's good," she says, and I know she means it. "You've been hurting."

So have you, I think, but I leave the words unsaid. My mother's grief is different than mine, and she is handling it her own way.

"So are you ready to come home? I'm sure I can catch a flight to Kamloops this evening. If we get a decent start in the morning, we could be back in Vancouver by late afternoon."

"Thanks, Mom. I really appreciate you and Reed taking time from your work to do this for me."

"No problem, sweetie. We don't mind at all. So it's settled then. Let me call the airline and —"

I don't let her finish. It's time to run the gauntlet. Taking a deep breath to fortify myself, I say, "The thing is I still have some stuff to do here."

Silence.

And then, "What kind of stuff?"

This is where things get tricky. If I don't explain my plans to meet Arlo in just the right way, my mother is going to go straight up and turn left. Actually, there's a good chance she'll do that anyway.

"Besides the property and truck, Sam left me some personal things. Not much, but one of —"

"What things?"

"I'll show you when I get home."

"Dani!"

I am amazed at how my name spoken in that authoritative, matriarchal tone can wield so much clout. Even half a province away, my mother still has the power.

"Okay," I concede. "He left his wallet, a letter from one of his foster families, a picture of himself as a little boy, and half a silver heart. Do you know anything about that?"

"A silver heart? No. At least not that I remember."

"So you don't have the other half of the heart?"

"No."

"I didn't think so," I mumble, "but I thought I'd ask."

Mom isn't easy to sidetrack. "So what do these things have to do with not coming home?"

"Well, Sam also left an address book. Most of the entries were business numbers, but there was also one for an Arlo Jones. So I called it and —"

"You did what!"

"I called the number. Don't have a hissy fit, Mother. I thought this guy might be able to tell me about Sam. Arlo was his friend, and he's agreed to talk to me. So tomorrow I'm going to Barriere to meet him."

"Have you lost your mind? This man is a total stranger."

That sets me back on my heels a bit. Yes, literally speaking, I suppose she's right. Arlo is a stranger, but because he was in Sam's address book, I just assumed he was an okay guy. Maybe I should have been more cautious, but there is no way I'm admitting that to my mom. "We're meeting in a public restaurant, Mother," I bluster as if she were being ridiculously protective. "Nothing is going to happen."

"Forget it, Dani. You're not going. I forbid it."

I know I shouldn't, but I burst out laughing. I can't help myself. I mean, there's no way she can stop me. She knows it too, and because it must hurt her to realize she can't make my decisions for me anymore, I say more kindly, "Mom, I'm not a little kid, and I don't do dumb things — well, not too often anyway. I need to know about Sam. Arlo can help me."

"Dani, please be reasonable. Sam was abandoned on a doorstep when he was a baby. There are no records. What do you think this Arlo can possibly tell you?"

"I don't know, but it's a place to start."

"Are you telling me you plan to turn this into a full-blown manhunt?"

Until she said that, I hadn't even considered the idea. All I wanted was to talk to Arlo. But if he told me something that opened another door, of course I would want to follow that lead.

And because I don't want to have this discussion again if that happens, I say, "I only had six weeks with Sam, Mom. For my whole life that's it. I wish it had been longer, but it wasn't. I'm trying not to blame you or Sam, but sometimes I can't help it. I feel so cheated. I loved him, Mom, but I know almost nothing about him. He was my father. Half of who I am came from him. How can I know who *I* am if I don't know who *he* was? I'll wonder my whole life. Can't you see that? I may come up empty, but I have to at least try, and since I don't have school until September, now is the perfect time to see what I can find out. Please don't try to stop me."

Chapter Six

I DON'T WANT TO BE LATE for my meeting with Arlo, so I give myself plenty of time to get to Barriere and actually arrive half an hour early. I find a table for two near a window, where I can see my car and also the restaurant entrance. When the waitress comes, I order herbal tea and a muffin. Then I wait.

The restaurant is humming. The parking lot is too — vehicles and people criss-crossing non-stop as if they were weaving a giant tapestry. It's a wonder there aren't some fender benders.

I watch for Arlo. Though I have no idea what I should be looking for, I'm pretty sure he won't be driving any of the semis that pull in. They park on the fringes of the lot, creating a corral around the smaller vehicles. I expect the drivers to be as big as their trucks, burly and unshaven with ball caps and tattoos, but mostly they look like regular guys. The only distinguishing feature they share is that they all look tired.

I check my watch: ten o'clock on the nose. And for no other reason than that, I decide the guy half-running, half-limping across the highway must be Arlo. When he steps inside the restaurant and starts scoping the place out, I'm sure of it. He might be looking for a vacant table, but I don't think so.

I raise my arm and wave. He zeroes in on me and something like recognition flickers in his eyes. Then he heads in my direction.

Along the way he calls to one of the waitresses and points to the table where I'm sitting. "A double-double, Shirley, when you've got a second."

She nods. "Sure thing, Arlo. I'll be right with ya."

Before he reaches me he gets waylaid by another patron, so he and the coffee arrive at the same time. He slips the waitress a couple of bills and gestures to my muffin and tea as well as his coffee.

Shirley bobs her head and leaves.

"You didn't need to do that," I say. "I could've paid."

"I'm sure you could've," Arlo replies, matter-of-fact, just like Sam. I can see why they were friends.

"Thank you," I say.

He nods.

I stick out my hand. "I'm Dani."

"Arlo," he says and shakes my hand. "How was your drive?"

"Good," I answer. "I got here faster than I thought I would."

He chuckles. "Does that mean you had to wait for the restaurant to open?"

I roll my eyes. "I wasn't *that* early."

There's silence as we both search our brains for what to say next.

"I guess I'm a bit of a surprise," I offer finally. "I don't think Sam told anyone he had a daughter."

He slurps his coffee. "Not me. That's for sure."

"Well, don't feel too bad," I say. "I didn't know either until this past summer."

He leans back in his chair and crosses his arms over his chest. The expression on his face is a mix of skepticism and curiosity. *Carry on. I'm listening,* it says.

"It was an agreement between Sam and my mother," I tell him. "They'd already split up when my mother realized she was pregnant. Sam wanted me to have a proper family, and he thought if he stayed in the picture, that wouldn't happen. So my mom married somebody else, and when I was born everybody thought that guy was my father. Until last summer, I did too, even though he and my mom split up when I was five, and he hasn't been a big part of my life since then."

Arlo nods like he understands, but I don't see how he can.

"Even though my mom had promised not to tell me about Sam, she kept in touch with him the whole time I was growing up. She made sure he knew about me. I just didn't know about *him*. Then he got cancer, and when he realized he wasn't going to beat it, he decided he wanted to see me. He still didn't want me to know who he was, though. Anyway, when my mother remarried last summer, I went to stay with him."

Arlo looks puzzled.

"Mom said Sam was my uncle, and that he'd been estranged from the family since before I was born. She said he'd only recently resurfaced."

"And you bought that story?"

I shrug. "I didn't really have a choice. Then when I met Sam and we hit it off, I didn't care." I shake my head. "When I think back on things, though, I should have been suspicious."

"Why's that?"

"There were so many red flags. Sam and my mother evading my questions. Old photos. Conflicting stories." I screw up my face as I remember. "Nothing big and in your face. You know? Just a whole lot of little stuff. So I just let it slide."

"How did you find out the truth?"

"It was a total accident. I was tidying up the trailer one day when I came across Sam's medicine. It scared me, so I phoned my mom for some answers. She said Sam had cancer. Then she phoned Sam to let him know I'd found out. That night he and I had a big heart-to-heart, and that's when he told me he was my dad."

There's another long pause as we both digest my words.

I crumple the muffin wrapper I've been fidgeting with and chuck it onto the plate. "Sometimes it makes me so angry I could scream," I say. "My mom and

Sam kept this huge secret from me — and for what? It was all so pointless. I found out anyway, but instead of having eighteen years with Sam, all I got was six weeks! I missed so much."

"I'm sure they thought they were doing what was best," Arlo says quietly.

My eyes are stinging. I offer him a wobbly smile. "What's that saying about the road to Hell?"

He doesn't say anything.

I take a deep breath and try another smile. "Your turn. How did you and Sam become friends?"

He drains the rest of his coffee and puts down his cup. "The rodeo circuit. I'd been on it a year when Sam started. We were both just kids." His eyes twinkle. "You bounce better when you're young. Anyway, because we were both green — not seasoned veterans like the other cowboys — we gravitated to each other and became friends."

My heart skips a couple of beats. "So you were around when Sam and my mom were together?"

He scratches his head and frowns. "There was this blonde who showed up from time to time for about a year, I guess." He squints at me. "Come to think of it, she looked kinda like you. I guess it could've been your mom."

"Sam didn't introduce you?"

Arlo chuckles. "Sam was pretty private, even back then."

I'm incredulous. "Didn't you ask?"

He shrugs. "There was no point. If he'd wanted me to know, he'd have told me."

I'm not sure if this *let-it-be* attitude is unique to Arlo and Sam or if it's a universal *guy* thing — all I know is it's maddening.

Arlo obviously doesn't pick up on my frustration, because he keeps on talking. "After that, I don't remember any other women. Oh, there were women, but nobody special."

"Did *you* ever marry?"

He shakes his head. "Rodeo life and family don't fit too well. Some fellas can make it work, but —" He leaves his sentence hanging and shrugs.

So far I haven't learned anything. I try a different approach. "The woman at the boarding house said Sam had something to do with you moving to Barriere."

Arlo snorts. "He had *everything* to do with it. A few years back, a bronc threw me. Nothing unusual about that, except that I landed too close to the horse's feet, and before I could roll out of the way, it stomped on my leg. Screwed up something in there pretty bad. Even after physio, it never righted itself. My bronc-riding days were over. But rodeo was all I knew, so I tried working as a rodeo clown — you know — the guy who draws the attention of the bulls and broncs away from the fallen riders."

I nod.

"But my bum leg wouldn't even allow me to do that. I couldn't move fast enough. I was more of a hindrance than a help. The rodeo had no choice but to let me go. After that, it was straight downhill. I had no skills, and I was feelin' pretty sorry for myself.

Within six months I'd drunk away any money I'd had. I was as down and out as they come."

He glances up from his cup and shakes his head. "I don't even like to remember." Then he breathes in deeply and continues. "Then Sam came looking for me. I don't know why — or how he even knew where to find me, but he did. He set me up at Nellie's Boarding House and got me going to Alcoholics Anonymous."

Arlo looks me straight in the eye. "I never slipped off the wagon — not even once. There was no way I was going to make Sam sorry he'd put himself out for me. I got a job as a custodian at a local community club. It didn't pay a lot, but it covered my board at Nellie's. It wasn't much of a life, but it was better than what I'd been living, and that's for sure.

"Then one day Sam shows up again and says we're going for a drive." Arlo gestures out the window. "He brought me here — to Barriere. He said he had this bitty piece of land with a trailer. An investment, he said, but he couldn't look after it, because of being away so much with the rodeo, and would I take care of it for him.

"Well, I'm no fool. I knew what Sam was doing. He was offering me a new life. He didn't say so, of course and neither did I. He even arranged a job for me at a gas station. After I'd been in Barriere a while, I got an envelope from a lawyer. It contained the deed for the property and trailer — and it was in my name."

My heart swells in my chest. I can't speak, so I don't even try.

"That's a true friend," Arlo says so softly that I almost don't hear him. He clears his throat. "I always thought I'd pay him back. I've been putting money away, whenever I have a few extra dollars. But now it's too late."

I find my voice, shaky as it is. "No, it's not, Arlo," I say. "You can pay it forward. Sam helped you. Somewhere down the line, you can help somebody else."

He's staring at his coffee cup again. "Yeah," he says. "Maybe. Someday. Who knows?"

"So do you like it here?" I ask, trying to lighten up the conversation.

He looks up and smiles. "I do. It's the first time since I left the circuit that I feel like I belong somewhere. The best part is that I'm involved in rodeo again. Not riding or anything like that. Now I'm one of the organizers — one of the behind-the-scenes guys who makes it all work. Turns out I know more about the business than I realized, and with my connections I can make things happen that other folks can't. It's a win-win situation for Barriere and me."

Arlo snickers. "Sam might have been a long, skinny drink of water, but there was a lot to him. He was sly. He could read people. He knew Barriere was what I needed."

"Sounds like you and Sam were best friends," I say.

"God, no." Arlo shakes his heads. "We were friends, for sure, but his best friend was always his horse — and that old truck of his."

"Lizzie." I smile.

Arlo looks surprised. "You know Lizzie?"

"It was Lizzie and Sam who taught me how to drive a standard transmission."

Arlo chuckles. "I remember when Sam bought that truck. Of course, it was a lot newer then."

"A lot redder too, I bet," I say.

He nods. "Yup. Lizzie was pretty red and shiny back then. So when she got the first dent in her tailgate, Sam was beside himself. Did he ever tell you about that?"

"No," I say, crossing my arms on the table and leaning forward.

"Well, he couldn't have had that truck more than about three months. Rodeo season was winding down, so Sam and I decided to do a little camping in the mountains to unwind. Anyway, we packed up the truck and away we went...."

The more Arlo talks, the more he seems to remember. When lunchtime rolls around, he's still going strong. So we have the soup and sandwich special, and this time I pick up the bill. We've been at the restaurant so long, I'm starting to think we're going to be asked to pay rent. Finally Arlo and I say our goodbyes, and as he limps across the highway back to his life, I turn my little Honda toward Kamloops.

Chapter Seven

DURING THE DRIVE BACK, I replay the morning in my head. I laughed a little, cried a little, and learned a lot. Arlo shared a ton of stories about Sam, and though they aren't experiences I was part of, I'll keep them with my memories.

Unfortunately, none of what I learned had anything to do with Sam's roots, which was the reason I wanted to talk to Arlo in the first place. As much as I don't want to admit it, my mother might be right. The clues to Sam's past could already be lost, and if that's true, all I'm doing is taking an unplanned tour of B.C.'s interior. If Sam never found out who his birth family was, what makes me think I'll uncover anything?

I let myself into my hotel room, flop onto the bed, and stare at the ceiling. So now what? Is this all there is? Do I just give up and head home to Vancouver? I tense, and the next thing I know, I'm back on my feet. I can't quit. Not yet. I've barely started searching. Half of my history is tied to Sam. The only way I'll ever know about me is to find out about him.

But I've already checked out all the clues. Haven't I? Though I'm probably wasting my time, I dig out the plastic bag containing Sam's belongings and go through it one more time. I study the half-heart. It means something. I'm sure of it; too bad I don't know what.

I reread the old letter from his foster family. There's no doubt these people cared about Sam. But why? He lived with a few different families. What made this one special? Why did he keep this letter? I look at the return address. I could use it to find a phone number. But the letter is twenty-two years old. Chances are the people don't even live there anymore. I frown and chew on my lip. Then I reach for my phone. There's one way to find out.

Back to the Canada White Pages. I do a search for Duncan Sheffield in Merritt. And there's the address — the same one as on the letter. The family is still there.

I dial the phone number listed. A woman answers. When I tell her who I am and why I'm calling, she is clearly stunned. She didn't know about Sam's death, and the knowledge obviously upsets her. Even so, she agrees to talk with me, and we arrange to meet at her home the next day.

And now for my mother. I can't imagine she'll be happy that I'm continuing with my search, but the fact that my investigation is taking me toward Vancouver should be some consolation. The conversation goes pretty much as I expect, and with a sigh of relief, I end the call. Bullet dodged. I wouldn't say Mom was thrilled with my plan, but she didn't try to talk me out of it.

———

I check out of my Kamloops hotel at nine thirty the next morning, and less than an hour later I'm checking into a motel in Merritt. It's the one my mom suggested. Considering she didn't make a fuss about me stopping in Merritt, I figure the least I can do is stay at a Joanna Malcolm–approved lodging. When I register, it turns out I already have a reservation. I shake my head and sigh. Clearly my mother isn't giving up her control of me without a fight.

After lunch it's time to meet the Sheffields. As I make my way to their home, the cheery female voice inside the GPS keeps me company, calling out directions and distances, and before I know it I'm there. "Drive 100 metres to destination on right," the GPS lady tells me.

"Already?" I say.

I'm fifteen minutes early, so I take note of the house, slide on by, and pull up around the corner to wait.

At precisely one o'clock, I'm standing on the sidewalk in front of the house. It's on a hill, and the driveway is fairly steep. I wouldn't want to tackle it when it's icy, but today is sunny and the pavement is dry, so it's not a problem. The yard is a series of tiered rock gardens. Considering it's only March, there isn't much happening in them except for some heather and the early shoots of tulips and daffodils. But the beds are free of weeds and the black earth has been freshly turned. It would appear these people enjoy gardening.

The house is older, but like the yard, it's well cared for. I climb the stairs leading to the front door and knock.

Almost immediately a man answers. He looks to be in his sixties. He's average height but thin, and his jeans and sweater hang shapelessly on his stork-like frame. His hair — what there is of it — circles his head like a silver laurel.

"Dani?" he says, swinging the door wide. His ice-blue eyes crinkle at the edges when he smiles.

I nod and smile back. "Yes."

"I'm Duncan Sheffield. It's nice to meet you. Please come in."

He takes my coat and leads me into the living room. *Whoa!* Floor to ceiling, it's one giant photo album.

He gestures to a chair, so I pull my gaze away from the photo-papered walls and sit down.

"How was your drive?" he asks.

"Good. The roads were clear, and there wasn't much traffic."

"Will you be going back today?"

I shake my head. "No. I've finished my business in Kamloops, and since I live in Vancouver, this is on the way home. I've checked into a motel. I'll stay there tonight," I shrug, "or longer, depending on what you and your wife can tell me about Sam."

"Speaking of my wife, I should let her know you're here. She's making tea." He winks. "I'll be right back. Make yourself comfortable."

At home, making myself comfortable would involve stretching out on the couch with a couple of cushions under my head, the remote in my hand, and a bowl of popcorn on the table beside me. Since that's not an option here — I don't even see a television — I check out the plethora of photographs decorating the walls. At first, I feel guilty about it, like I'm snooping, but then I decide that's crazy. Why would people plaster the room with photos if they didn't want anyone looking at them?

The photographs are mostly of people, who I assume are family — several generations worth by the look of it. I recognize Duncan Sheffield in many of them, joined often by an equally thin woman, probably his wife, and a girl, who varies in age with each picture. Though there's something mesmerizing about these photos, as if they were windows into these people's lives, I keep hoping to stumble upon Sam. But since the photos are in no specific order, I have no way of knowing where to look. And Sam may not be there anyway.

I stop at a large sepia portrait of a man and woman. Judging by their clothing and the formal setting, I'm guessing the picture dates back to the early 1900s. The couple look to be in their twenties, and though they are as sombre as two people can be, I know that was the style of photos for that time, and I can't help wondering if they became animated after their picture was taken. Did the woman smile and giggle? Did the man spin his hat on his walking stick? Did they —

"My great-grandparents," a woman says behind me, and I whirl around. "I'm sorry," she says. "I didn't mean to startle you. I'm Stephanie Sheffield." She offers me her hand.

"Dani Lancaster," I say. Though I've just come in from outside, the cold of her touch is startling. Even more startling are her eyes. They are like pieces of shiny coal. She smiles, and her face becomes a roadmap of lines. And suddenly she's pretty. Her personality is written in those lines, and they say she is a compassionate, loving person — and what is prettier than that?

"You don't look like Sam," she says, and I realize she's been studying me too.

"People say I'm like my mother."

She gestures to the couch. "Sit down." Then she and her husband sit on the loveseat opposite.

"Tea?" she asks, lifting the pot from the tray on the coffee table separating us.

"That would be nice. Thank you."

She passes me a china cup decorated with flowers and trimmed with gold. It's so delicate I can almost see through it. I set the teacup down in front of me and add sugar and lemon. Stephanie and Duncan add milk to theirs. Then we all sit back.

It is Stephanie who begins. "I confess that when you called yesterday and told me Sam was —" she pauses and looks flustered, "— that Sam had passed away, I was shocked and upset. He lived with us from the time he was fifteen until after he graduated from high school. He could have stayed even after that, but he felt obligated to leave."

I frown. "Why?"

"Social services only pays for foster care until the youth turns eighteen," Duncan says. "So Sam felt he was putting us out."

"Is that why he joined the rodeo?"

"More or less," he says. "He worked part-time for a while and paid us board."

"He insisted," Stephanie cuts in. "We didn't want to take his money, but he was adamant about paying his way."

Duncan takes over again. "Sam had always loved animals, horses especially. One of his other foster homes was a farm. That's where he learned to ride."

"And work," Stefanie grumbles. "Those people worked him so hard. They had several foster children and they treated them all like slaves. Instead of hiring help, they took in foster kids. That way they had free labour and got paid besides. It makes me so angry when I think how that couple used those children. As if they hadn't had a hard enough life as it was."

Duncan pats his wife's hand. "Don't get yourself all worked up, Steph. It wasn't as bad as all that. Yes, the kids had gruelling chores, but they weren't abused. And Sam came away with a good work ethic as well as the skills that would lead him to his life's career."

Stephanie clucks her tongue. "You are being too kind, Duncan."

"Have you always taken in foster children?" I ask.

Stephanie shakes her head. "Sam was our only one. He went to school with our daughter. We had met him at a few school functions, and so when Debbie, our daughter, told us Sam's foster family was sending him back to social services, we volunteered to take him in. Never once did he make us sorry."

"Do you know anything about his background — the foster families he stayed with before, or his birth parents?"

Duncan answers. "We know of the foster family who owned the farm, but they no longer live in the area. I don't know where they moved. Other than that, all we have is the information Social Services provided when Sam came to us. He was a foundling left on a doorstep in Farrow. That's a small community not far from here."

"Do you know the name of the people he was left with?"

Stephanie and Duncan exchange glances. "According to social services, it was an elderly couple," Duncan says. "But they died a long time ago."

Though I nod, I feel my hopes plummeting. Another dead end. And I was so hoping I would find a clue here. I look around the room. "Do you —" I lick my lips and start again. "I probably shouldn't ask this, but you have so many photographs. Do you ... do you have any of Sam that I could have?"

Again, Stephanie and Duncan exchange glances. "I'm sorry, Dani," Stephanie says. "I've been so caught up in my own loss that I haven't thought about how you must feel." She gets up, lifts a photograph from the wall, and offers it to me. "Sam and our daughter, Debbie," she says. "It was taken at a baseball tournament. Sam's team was in the provincial championship."

I gaze at the photograph. It's Sam, all right, though a much younger version. Not the middle-aged cowboy I knew but a teenage baseball player. And though it doesn't matter, I ask, "Did he win?"

Chapter Eight

THE SHEFFIELDS ARE NICE PEOPLE, and I appreciate that they met with me and told me what Sam was like as a teenager. I'm grateful for the photograph too, of course, but as far as information that will help me find Sam's birth mother, they told me nothing — except the name of the town where he was left as a baby.

So it's back to Google.

"Farrow is a small unincorporated village located in the Nicola Valley region of British Columbia about 40 kilometres southeast of Merritt," I read aloud. *"It dates back to the gold rush of the 1860s, when prospectors trickling out of the Kootenays reportedly discovered gold in a stream there. This brought more gold seekers, and when deposits of silver, copper, and coal were also discovered, mining potential provided a basis for settlement. Farrow was named after the first mining*

company to stake a claim. The installation of a feeder line to the Kettle Valley Railway in nearby Brookmere provided a means of transporting the mined minerals to major centres and as a result the town grew.

"During its boom years, the village boasted a drugstore, bank, church, and hotel, as well as an assortment of small stores and other businesses. Around 1950, Farrow's population peaked at nearly 2,000.

"In recent years the village has dwindled to a handful of residents, rendering it little more than a ghost town. Located less than a mile east of Highway 5, Farrow is accessible via a gravel road."

I put down the phone, sag against my chair, and sigh. Sure, I could drive to Farrow. But what's the point if there's no one there to answer my questions?

I try to look on the bright side. It would be just as hard — maybe harder — to get answers if I were somewhere like Toronto. Then there would be too many people. Besides, it's not like Farrow is totally deserted. People still live there — a few, anyway. And the ones who have stayed are probably the diehards, the people who have a history with the place — the ones who might be able to answer my questions.

What have I got to lose?

———

I check out of the motel and inhale the sunny spring morning all the way to my toes before sliding into my little Honda.

"Let's go, Gloria," I say as I turn the key in the ignition. "Gloria" is the name I've given the lady in my GPS. "I hope you've had your coffee, because we need to have a good day." Then it dawns on me that I'm talking to my GPS just like Sam used to talk to his truck. At first it startles me, but then I think of it as another thread binding us together, and the idea pleases me.

I have the highway more or less to myself. It's the grey season, that bleak time of year after winter has released its stranglehold but before spring has had a chance to kick in, and though the fir trees are green and the sky is blue, everything else is grey. The rock embankments, the grass, the distant hills — everything. It's as if the world is coated with a dull film and Mother Nature needs to hose it away to make everything fresh and new.

Along the highway are *point of interest* signs indicating station stops along the old Kettle Valley Rail Line. These are names of characters from Shakespearean plays. Apparently one of the engineers had a passion for the Bard. According to the map, the turnoff for Farrow is just south of the marker for Juliet, so as soon as I pass it — even though I trust Gloria to tell me where to turn — I slow down and keep my eyes peeled for the exit.

"Keep left," Gloria directs me and then adds, "In 450 metres, turn left."

"Gotcha," I say, spotting the left turn lane ahead. I check my rear-view mirror, put on my turn signal, and change lanes.

As I wait for the oncoming traffic to go by, I squint at the sign tacked to a post at the entrance to the road — a barn board someone has written on. The white paint is so cracked and faded, I can barely make out the letters. I'm pretty sure they spell "Farrow," but maybe that's because it's what I expect to be there.

The article on the Internet said the road was gravel. It is — in some places anyway. In other parts the gravel is long gone, and what passes for a road is a collection of potholes and ruts that bounce me past an orchard of gnarled old fruit trees, a dilapidated barn that's leaning so much I could blow it over and a sign warning visitors not to drink the water.

Gloria seems to be weathering the bumpy ride better than I am because her voice is as steady and cheerful as ever when she announces, "In 100 metres, destination on right." Then a few seconds later, "Destination on right."

I slow to a crawl and peer out the passenger window. There's another sign, just as ancient as the one at the highway, but at least I can read this one. *Welcome to Farrow.* I glance around. Okay, I'll bite. Where?

I move on, rolling slowly over the rutted road like a rowboat in a stormy sea. Straight ahead is a crossroad, and it's paved. Main Street, according to the signpost. I glance both ways. There's not a car in sight. Buildings line the sides of the road, but they're in pretty rough shape. Most are boarded up, and the ones that aren't look like they should be.

The place is totally deserted. Or is it? Half a block away, I see a dog. It pads from my side of the road to the other and scratches at the door of a white storefront. Almost immediately, the door opens and an elderly man shuffles out. He pats the dog and the two make their way to a patch of sun farther down the sidewalk. The man lowers himself into a chair and starts to rock. The dog curls up beside him.

I ease my car onto Main Street, cover the half block, and park. As I step onto the street, I can feel the man watching me. When I cross the road, the dog lifts its head.

I smile. "Good morning."

The man nods but says nothing. The dog starts to get up, but when the man strokes its back, it grumbles and settles down again.

The man shades his eyes and squints at me. "Lose your way?" he says. "We don't get many visitors here in Farrow. Do we, Ralphie?"

The dog's tail thumps the sidewalk.

"Actually, I'm looking for someone," I tell him.

"You don't say. And who might that be? I know most everybody hereabouts. Down to Brookmere too." He gestures to an overturned milk crate. "Set yourself down and tell me who you're lookin' for. Is it the Moyers? They get the most company. Mind you, none of 'em stays long. But then nobody does. Farrow's not exactly New York City, if you know what I mean." He grins, and a gold tooth glints in the sunlight. "It used to be a sight more lively back in the old days, but when the mine shut down — and the railway too — there was nothing to keep folks here. Too bad, cuz it's a nice little town."

I glance around skeptically.

"Oh, I know it don't look like much, but there's nothin' that a hammer and nails and a lick of paint couldn't fix. It ain't looks that make a place anyway; it's the people."

I nod and sit on the milk crate. "So how many people live here?"

He screws up his face in thought. "On a good day, one hundred fifty maybe. If Bobby and Linda Matlock are bickering, Linda will be gone to stayin' with her sister in Kelowna, and then there just be one hundred forty-nine. Mostly it's older folk like me, cuz we don't need jobs. We got our pensions. The younger folk who live here — they stay cuz they can't afford anything else. Property's cheap. Some of them inherited land too. They all work somewhere else though — mostly Merritt."

I nod again and point towards the rutted road. "When I was driving in, I saw a sign that said there was no drinking water. How do you manage?"

"We truck water in. Use that for drinking, and use stream and well water for most everything else. The water situation is fixable too, but Farrow folk can't afford to do anything, and the government jus' wants to forget we're here. The faster the town dies out, the happier they'll be. There ain't nothing we can do about it either. Nobody but us cares, and one hundred fifty people — one hundred forty-nine if Linda Matlock's off sulking — can't make much noise."

As I think about what the man has said, I turn my face to the warm morning sun and open myself to my surroundings. Though I'm in downtown Farrow and the highway is less than a mile away, I feel swallowed up by nature. It's the same feeling I used to get sitting in the meadow at Sam's place.

The man interrupts my thoughts. "So who is it you've come to see?"

Suddenly I remember that I don't know the name of the old couple who took Sam in. Perhaps he took their last name. "Swan?" I answer hesitantly.

He scratches his head and frowns. "You don't know?"

"Not for sure. What I do know is that they were an older couple in the 1970s and they would have had a little boy living with them."

The man's face clears. "Well, why didn't you say so? Here I was thinkin' you were lookin' for someone by that name now, and there just ain't no one. You're talkin' about old John and Hannah Swan. Good people, them two. Real good people. O' course, they're long dead now — buried in the local cemetery — but, yeah, they lived here their whole lives. And, if I recollect rightly, their niece's son lived with them for a few years. Then one day he was gone. Never did find out what happened there."

Another dead end. I sigh and stand up. "Thanks," I say.

"What'd you want with John and Hannah anyway?" he asks.

I shrug. "That little boy was my father. He was

left on the Swans' doorstep when he was a baby. I was hoping that coming here might lead me to his birth mother."

The man's eyebrows shoot up. "Well, I'll be jiggered. Just shows you what a body don't know. I was a lot younger then. The Swans woulda been my parents' age. I didn't know them real well except to say hello, but I know where they lived. I could give you directions, if you'd like."

I know I'm grasping at straws, but that's all I've got. "I would like that very much," I say.

Chapter Nine

I FEEL LIKE I'M STANDING in a minefield after the war. The remains of basements scar the scraggly field like ragged concrete craters and the ground is littered with tree stumps, shards of glass, rusty nails, and chunks of rotting wood. I carefully pick my way around the debris.

I shouldn't be walking here. The area is surrounded by a chain link fence that sports an intimidating padlock and a big KEEP OUT sign. But since one panel has been ripped away, offering an alternate entrance, I use it.

The old man said the area was earmarked for a housing development in the 1980s, but the project never got off the ground. After buying out the homeowners and tearing down the houses, the developer ran out of money, and the government claimed the property for unpaid taxes.

I don't even know which basement belonged to John and Hannah Swan. I wander from crater to crater, peering into them, hoping to see something that is Sam. But except for algae, puddles of stagnant water, and crushed drink cans, the basements are empty. I want to believe that when I come to the right foundation, it will speak to me.

But it doesn't, and the reality is disheartening.

I'm running out of leads. I have only one more place to check out: the cemetery. The old man gave me directions for that too, so I fish the paper I wrote them on from my pocket and head back to my car.

———

Still reeling from the condition of the abandoned housing development, I expect the cemetery to be neglected and overgrown, but it's actually picturesque. There is no church beside it nor any sort of administration building — not even a maintenance shed. All that sets it apart from its rustic surroundings is a freshly painted white picket fence. There is no sign to identify it, no gate either, just a modest opening wide enough to accommodate pallbearers and a coffin. There isn't even a walkway, just grass and graves. The cemetery has no pretensions. It is what it has always been, what it was intended to be: a final resting place for the people of Farrow.

The headstones are arranged in orderly rows, so I walk their length, looking for John and Hannah Swan. I find them in the fifth row. They are buried side by side. Their places are marked by simple stone crosses engraved with their names and pertinent dates. John died first; Hannah followed three months later. Though I write down the dates, I doubt they will be much help.

But there is something that might. The graves share a vase of flowers. They aren't fresh, but they aren't wilted either, which means they were placed here recently. The question is, by whom? If someone cares enough about these people to place flowers on their thirty-year-old graves, that person might also know about Sam. A spark of hope flares inside me.

And that's when I hear a loud whirring. I glance around. Across the cemetery, I see a young woman trimming the grass around the headstones. I didn't notice her before, so she must have arrived after me. I peer towards the road. Sure enough, there's an old, beat-up truck parked behind my car.

I jog across the graveyard.

"Excuse me. Excuse me," I yell and wave my arms.

The young woman shuts off the weed whacker, lifts the safety muffs from her ears, and frowns in my direction.

"Can you help me?" I ask.

She shrugs. "What do you want?"

I point to the other end of the cemetery. "A couple of graves over there — John and Hannah Swan — have flowers. Do you know who put them there?"

She shakes her head. "I just do maintenance. I'm not the cemetery's social convener."

Her unfriendly manner sets me back on my heels. I try again. "Have flowers been left there before?"

She pulls off her protective glasses and glares at me, and I realize she's probably not much older than I am. "Why do you want to know?"

"I'm looking for someone, and the person who put the flowers there might be able to help me."

She snorts and shakes her head. "Like I already said, I don't poke my nose into other people's business. A woman changes the flowers every Saturday afternoon. That's all I know."

"Saturday afternoon. You're sure?"

"No, I made it up. Of course, I'm sure. I wouldn't have said so if I wasn't." She puts her protective glasses and earmuffs back on. Our conversation is clearly over.

I thank her, but she doesn't hear. Saturday. That's only two days from now. If I can talk with that woman, I might learn something. I could go back to the motel in Merritt for a couple more nights, but I'd rather stay in Farrow and do more digging. I know there's no motel here, but maybe there's a bed and breakfast.

The girl has gone back to her weed whacking, so I wave my arms wildly to draw her attention again.

There's no mistaking the annoyance on her face as she once more shuts down her machine and removes her ear muffs. "What now?"

I refuse to let her surly attitude deter me. "Is there anywhere in town to rent a room?"

"The Apple Tree," she offers impatiently. It's on Fourth Avenue off Main." And without another word, she slips her earmuffs back on and resumes her work.

———

Thank God Farrow is small. I know where Main Street is, and if Fourth Avenue runs off it, I can find it. But I don't head there right away. Instead I drive around, checking out the various roads. Most of the shops on Main Street are run-down and closed, but the parts of town that still have a pulse are well cared for. Like Webb's River, there is more to Farrow than first meets the eye. It's layered, and you have to peel away those layers to get to its heart.

I find that heart at the crossroad of Second Avenue and another unnamed street that winds into the trees in one direction and into open fields in the other. According to the sign, it's the Farrow Community Hall. The building is old, but its wooden siding is painted a cheerful blue trimmed with white, and it immediately draws me in, so I stop for a closer look.

The front doors of the building are locked, but there's a glass-covered bulletin board and I read the notices on it. Everything from children's play groups and badminton clubs to yoga classes and line dancing are offered. The community hall is a busy place. But it's the poster advertising the upcoming Spring Bazaar that catches my eye. It's this Saturday. That means a gathering of the locals — people who might know something about Sam. It's exactly what I need, and since I'm going to stay to talk to the flower lady anyway, I can kill two birds with one stone.

Invigorated at the prospect of making a breakthrough, I practically skip around the outside of the building. Behind the hall is a playing field outfitted with bleachers, a backstop, and goal posts.

On the far side is a swing set, slide, and sandbox, and beyond that a large fenced corral, though it looks like it's been a while since it's seen any activity.

———

The girl at the cemetery didn't give me an exact address, but I have no problem locating The Apple Tree. It's nestled between two larger homes on Fourth Avenue and has a lone apple tree in the front yard. A carved sign swinging from a post confirms it's the place, though I'm not sure if the sign is intended to identify the tree or the pretty little cottage cozied in behind it.

There is no driveway, so I park on the grassy verge and follow a path of stepping stones to the front door.

It opens even before I knock, and a round, elderly woman steps into the opening. She's wearing a bib apron over a house dress, and her white hair is tied back in a stubby ponytail. As she stands there, a swarm of wonderful cooking smells rushes past her, and my stomach, not having seen food for several hours, growls ferociously. I gasp and slap my hand over it.

"Come for lunch, have you?" the woman says, and though she doesn't crack a smile, her eyes are twinkling.

I grimace. "I'm sorry. I didn't know my stomach was going to do that. I'm so embarrassed."

The woman chuckles. "Embarrassed because you're hungry? Fiddle-faddle. Save that for when your knickers fall around your ankles at a busy bus stop."

We both grin.

"Thank you," I say.

"So what can I do you for, young lady?"

"I was told I could find a room to rent for a few days."

She smiles. "And so you can. I charge seventy-five dollars a night. Cash only. That includes breakfast and supper. You're on your own for lunch." She glances at my stomach. "Except today. Come in." She tugs me inside.

"I'm George Washington," she says, leading me through to the kitchen. She pulls a chair out from the table and gestures for me to sit. "It's actually Georgina, but the only one who ever called me that was my grandmother. To everyone else, I've always been George." She puts a hand to her heart. "I cannot tell a lie." Then she doubles over with laughter.

I nod and smile. "I get it. That's why the apple tree."

She dabs her eyes with the corner of her apron and allows herself a few more chuckles. "If you have a moniker like mine, you have to make the most of it. It should have been a cherry tree," she shrugs, "but you have to work with what you've got. So who might you be?"

"Nobody so interesting as you," I say. "Just plain Dani Lancaster."

"Well, plain Dani Lancaster, what brings you to Farrow?"

I tell her. When I'm done, I say, "Did you know Sam?"

Her eyes get misty. "I did," she nods. "He was such a sweet little boy. And with those black eyes and dark curly hair, he was a real cutie-pie too. It broke Hannah's heart to cut those curls. You know, I don't think I've ever seen a more thoughtful child — certainly never one as curious. Sam was always asking questions. Would the grass grow forever if you didn't cut it? How high is up? Where does the sun go at night? He needed to know everything. God bless me, but that boy could drive a body to distraction with all his questions. Not John and Hannah, though. They had the patience of Job. When Sam asked a question, they answered it. For them the sun rose and set on that child."

"The Swans never told anyone the truth about how Sam came to live with them?"

George shakes her head. "Not a word. As far as anybody knew, Sam was their niece's son."

"George," I say, "were there any pregnant girls in Farrow at that time?"

She nods. "Yes, as a matter of fact, there was. One."

I lean forward hopefully. "There was? Who?"

She stirs a pot on the stove. "Me." Then she adds quickly, "But I'm not Sam's mother. I had a son when Sam was about a month old. And I kept him. Biggest mistake of my life. His name is Sebastien, and let me tell you, his name is the only good thing about him. He cleaned out my bank account two years ago, and I haven't seen him since. Here's hoping my luck holds."

Chapter Ten

ON FRIDAY MORNING, I drive to Merritt. I need money to pay for my room at The Apple Tree, and I also need some cash in case I want to buy something at Saturday's bazaar. As I wait in line for my turn at the ATM, a poster tacked to a bulletin board catches my eye. It's the same as the one at the community hall — the one advertising the bazaar. I'm surprised. I didn't realize Farrow's reach extended beyond the town's borders.

It's nearing noon when I finish my business, so I decide to grab something to eat before heading back. As I push open the door to a coffee shop, I spy another poster in the front window. When I pop into a drugstore for shampoo, there's one there too.

On my return drive, I see a huge sign that says *64th Annual Spring Bazaar in Farrow, Saturday,*

March 22nd. Don't miss it! That certainly wasn't there before. I start to get the feeling that the spring bazaar is a big deal.

I know George is at the community hall setting up, so I drop in to see if she needs help. From the look of it, every last resident of Farrow is there. I'm tempted to make inquiries about Sam, but everyone is so busy, they probably wouldn't welcome the interruption. According to the diagram on the wall, there is a carefully laid out plan for all the booths and exhibits, but you wouldn't know it from the chaos. The place is a giant mishmash of boxes, tables, electrical cords, balloons, banners, props, merchandise, and bodies.

I hear George before I see her. She whistles to get my attention. Her table is on the fringes, so I dodge some little kids playing tag and slide around a couple of men carting what looks like a miniature swimming pool, and make my way over.

"It's crazy busy in here," I say. "Do you need a hand?"

"That would be wonderful." She smiles wearily and drags the back of her hand across her forehead. Then she takes a deep breath and shakes the folds out of a big blue gingham cloth.

I catch an end of the billowing fabric and between us we spread it over the table.

"Looks good." I nod. "Very homey."

George waves away the compliment. "Hopefully it will be when we're done." She lifts a chicken-wire crate onto the table and angles it on its side near one end. Then she pushes a bulging green garbage bag toward me.

"What's this?"

"Hay," she says. "We want to stuff some into the crate — decorative-like, if you know what I mean. You can spill a little onto the table too. Makes a nice display for the jams and jellies."

"What's your best seller?" I ask.

She gestures to a long cardboard sign on the wall behind the table. *George's Fruit Jars: Sweet & Savoury Preserves. Best Apple Butter in B.C.*

"Do you offer samples?"

She blinks in surprise. "In all the years I've been doing this, the thought never crossed my mind. What a good idea!" Suddenly rejuvenated, her eyes sparkle with genuine excitement. "Let's get this finished. I have to get home and bake some bread."

———

That night I sleep like I've been drugged, and when I wake up the next morning, George is gone. There's a key and a note on the kitchen table.

I'm at the bazaar. Fresh baked muffins in the basket on the counter.

    Orange juice in the fridge. If you want something else, help yourself. Please lock up when you go out.

— George

I check the time. It's already nearly ten o'clock! The bazaar started an hour ago. I quickly down a glass of juice and grab a muffin to go.

Two blocks from the community hall, the road is already lined with vehicles on both sides. It's even more congested at the hall. Luckily for me, a car pulls out just as I approach, and I snag a spot directly across the street from the front door.

In the foyer, there's a table manned by two elderly women. Between them is a very large glass bowl and a sign that says, *Admission by donation*. Inside the bowl there's a healthy assortment of coins and bills. I fish a five from my wallet and drop it in.

"Thank you, dear," smiles one of the old ladies. She tears twin tickets off a roll, drops one into a decorated metal wastebasket, and hands me the other. "Keep this safe now," she says. "You could win a prize." She gestures to an impressive display of items behind her. "The draws will be made at three o'clock, so be sure you're here."

I thank her and move into the main room of the hall. It is totally transformed from what it was yesterday. Now the tables, booths, and other displays are arranged in orderly rows, decked with colourful signs and mountains of sale items. The aisles between are brimming with shoppers. There are easily three hundred people.

I ease my way into the crowd and am instantly swallowed up. I smell fresh-brewed coffee and suddenly remember that I haven't had mine yet. I spy the coffee urn a few tables away, but the crowd is moving at a snail's pace, and there's no way to push through, so I busy myself examining the wares until coffee is within reach. In no time I'm so absorbed with what I'm looking at and the people I'm talking to that I completely forget about coffee.

The bazaar has something for everyone. For culinary types there are spices, recipe books, aprons, fridge magnets, and pot holders. For those who are more interested in eating there's a popcorn machine and a doughnut-making machine, as well as several tables selling fudge and baked goods. There's stained glass, handmade quilts, homemade soap, candles of every shape, size, and colour, garden sculptures, paintings, stuffed toys, baby clothes, stationery, and puppets. Several tables are selling jewellery, so I buy a bracelet for my mother and earrings for myself. I can't leave Reed out, so I buy him some of George's preserves. Apple butter for sure, as well as blackberry jam, strawberry compote, and red pepper jelly. The old man I met the day I arrived in Farrow is selling intricately carved walking sticks. They are so beautiful I wish I had a reason to buy one. In addition to the items for sale, there are displays strategically placed among the tables: a photo history of the village, a collection of town artifacts, and a diorama of a long-ago mining operation.

There is so much to see, I can barely take it all in. The people manning the tables all have a story to tell, and I quickly realize how close everyone in the community is. The town may not be much to look at, and it may not have a large population, but its roots run deep and its residents are like a large family.

A pottery table is last, which is a good thing, because if I'd seen it when I first came in, I might have spent half my inheritance at it. Even though the morning isn't over, most of the pieces remaining have "sold" stickers.

"Oh, my god," I gush. "Everything is so beautiful." Different than anything I've seen before. "Is it all done on a wheel?"

The young woman behind the table nods. "Mostly. There are a few pieces of slab work, though nothing here right now." She shrugs. "Sorry. We had no idea the pottery would be so popular. We didn't bring enough, but we'll be restocking for the afternoon."

"Really? I'd love to buy a piece. Do you have any more bowls like this one?" I run my fingers around the rim, thinking of my mom. She could use some of these pieces in her interior design business.

"Similar, yes. Each piece is individually crafted, so no two are exactly the same, but I'm sure we have something you'll like. The new stock should be here by one o'clock." I glance at my watch. It's almost eleven thirty. I have to leave in half an hour if I want to catch up with the flower lady at the cemetery.

I bite my lip. "Unfortunately, I have an appointment, and I don't know how long it'll take. Do you have a business card? Your work is gorgeous, and if I can't get something today, maybe I could get hold of you after the bazaar."

"Oh, I'm not the potter," she says quickly. "I'm just helping out. But I'll pass your compliments along." She ducks down under the table, and when she pops up again, she hands me a green embossed card. "Here you go," she smiles, "in case you don't get back."

"Thanks very much." According to the card, Alex Burke is the potter. I stuff the card into my pocket.

Exit Here, reads a huge sign over a set of open double doors at the back of the hall, so I head toward them. On the way I see a fishing pool for kids. There's no water in it, just plastic pellets and tiny toys encased in bags sealed with metal clips. The children are armed with fishing rods dangling magnetic bait. If squeals and giggles are any indication, they're all having a good time and even catching a few toys.

As I step outside I pass a dunk tank just as a young man wings a baseball at the target, sending the pretty girl perched on the platform plunging into the water. The mini playground is in full use, and a half-dozen kids are kicking a soccer ball around the field. The bazaar organizers clearly planned for kids. They also thought about lunch. Several barbecues are set up, churning out mouth-watering smells of hotdogs and hamburgers.

"Five minutes." One of the chefs raises an open hand.

I nod and smile. "I'll be back," I say and head over to the corral, which — unlike the last time I saw it — is in full use. Ponies carrying little kids parade in a circle, each one led by a cowboy or cowgirl. On the outside of the corral, the next round of riders impatiently awaits its turn.

I lean on the fence to watch. It takes me back to Webb's River and my riding lessons at Greener Pastures Ranch.

A voice interrupts my thoughts. "You a rider?"

I look around at the ancient cowboy standing at my shoulder. Where did he come from?

"I've done a little, but I'm not very good," I tell him. "Twice around the corral, and these little people will be better than me."

He chuckles. "Kids are naturals. I been working with them most of my life. My son and his wife raise horses down the highway a few miles. I live with them. I used to rent this corral and offer riding lessons, but as more and more folks moved away, I just couldn't make money at it."

My heart does a mini flip. Could Sam have taken riding lessons from this man? The cowboy answers my question before I even ask it.

"Of course, I wasn't here when Farrow was really in its heyday. That would've been mid fifties, and I didn't move here until '93."

My hopes do a nosedive.

"Farrow was dying even then, but it was still a nice little town. Hard to believe now," he says, "but there was a time when this corral was busy all the time. There used to be a barn and a grandstand right over there." He points across the way.

"Why a grandstand?"

"Rodeo. It was a good one too. But that died out like everything else in this town. It's a shame. It's a real shame. But the truth is, this is probably the last time this corral will get used for anything."

I frown. "Why do you say that?"

"Every year more people move away. The bazaar has always drawn a big crowd, but it's a lot of work to organize, especially when there aren't many bodies to do it. It's been around for sixty-four years, but this is the last time. It's a real shame, I tell you."

Chapter Eleven

THOUGH IT'S ONLY 12:20 when I get to the cemetery, I'm worried that the flower lady has already been and gone. I hurry to the graves of John and Hannah Swan to find out.

There are no fresh flowers, and I breathe a sigh of relief.

But by one o'clock, the woman still hasn't shown up, so I start reading the headstones to pass the time. Most of my friends think graveyards are scary — or at least morbid. They imagine bodies devoured by maggots and worms, or decaying zombies pushing up through the ground to attack the living. I, on the other hand, find cemeteries peaceful. There's something comforting about walking among people who are at rest.

By two thirty I'm familiar enough with the graveyard to conduct tours. I know that Barnaby

Wacker's grave is the oldest and Melanie Dufresne's is the most recent. I know William Hornby Jr. was the youngest person to die — four hours old — and Mable Myerson lived to be 101. I know Drake Hodges was killed during a dispute over a mining claim and the entire Foligno family died in a house fire. Just by reading the markers I have a sense of who lived full and satisfying lives, the people who were much-loved, and the ones who life cheated in some way or another.

A fat raindrop splatters the back of my hand, and I look up. The sky is thick with black clouds. I don't know when they arrived, but they don't look like they plan on leaving any time soon.

Splat, splat, splat, splat! As they seriously begin to dump their load, I scurry for my car. I'm barely inside when the sky opens up like the Hoover Dam. The rain pelts down for a good fifteen minutes, bouncing off the hood and windshield like liquid buckshot, and then, suddenly used up, it stops, and a laser beam of sunlight punches a hole in the grey, exposing a lonely little patch of blue.

Through my rear-view mirror I see a car pull up behind me. The driver, a woman, turns off the engine and reaches behind her, retrieving a bouquet of flowers before exiting the vehicle.

She has to be the flower lady.

I want to jump out of my Honda and run over to her before she can even close her car door, but no doubt she'd think I'm a lunatic, so I force myself to stay where I am.

I wait until she's through the fence. Then I casually let myself out of my car and stroll after her, making sure to keep a reasonable distance between us. Until she stops at the graves of John and Hannah Snow, that is. Then I can't contain myself any longer.

"Excuse me," I call as I jog towards her.

She's on her haunches, reaching for the wilted bouquet, but she glances curiously over her shoulder. "Pardon?"

I force myself back to a walk. "Sorry to bother you. I wonder if you could help me."

"Car trouble?" she says, looking past me toward the Honda. "I saw you sitting there when I drove up."

I shake my head and smile. "No, it's not that." I point to the graves. "It's about John and Hannah Swan."

She looks back at their graves, places the new bouquet of flowers in the recessed vase, and stands up. Then she looks back at me and cocks her head quizzically. "What about them?"

"Are they your family?"

Her eyes narrow. "Why do you ask?"

I take a step back. The last thing I want is to spook her. "Because my father was left on their doorstep when he was a baby," I blurt. "I'm trying to find out why he was abandoned and who his mother was. I want to know who his family was — who my family is." I gesture to the fresh bouquet and shrug. "You leave flowers for them, so I thought you might know something."

The woman smiles sadly and shakes her head. "I'm sorry," she says. "I don't know these people. In fact, I don't know anyone in Farrow. I'm a florist. I have a shop in Merritt. I'm paid to change the flowers each week. I've been doing it for years."

It takes a few seconds for her words to sink in. "Really?" I blink. "Someone pays you to do this? Can you tell me who?" This could be the breakthrough I've been waiting for.

She shakes her head again. "I'm afraid not. To be honest, I don't know myself. All I can tell you is that every six months I get a bank draft for a half year's worth of flowers." She sighs. "But I'm afraid that's coming to an end. A month ago I received a letter from a lawyer in Kamloops, informing me that the person paying for the flowers had died."

My knees instantly turn to jelly. It's a wonder they continue to hold me up.

I watch in a daze as the woman stuffs the wilted bouquet into a plastic bag and ties it shut. "So that's that. My golden goose has flown the coop." She sighs. "Aw, well, I shouldn't complain. It was great while it lasted." As she heads towards her car, she calls back, "Good luck with your search. Sorry I couldn't help."

I don't reply. I'm still too stunned. Sam was the person who arranged for the flowers to be placed at the graves. It had to be him. It's the only logical explanation. He probably set it up through Bob Morgan. I can check with the lawyer, but I really don't need to. I know in my heart it's the truth. It's such a Sam thing to do.

I kneel down. Some of the flowers in the bouquet are stuck together, so I gently separate them and turn them to show off their blooms. I smile.

"He loved you guys," I tell Hannah and John, in case they didn't already know.

It's after three o'clock. The bazaar will be winding down, but I might still be able to purchase a piece of pottery, so I hop back into my car and head back. At least I think I'm heading back, but my mind is still at the cemetery, thinking about what the florist told me. Somehow I make the wrong turn and before I know it I'm driving into unknown territory. Trees and bush spring up out of nowhere and the paved road narrows into a dirt track, making it impossible to turn around. It's muddy too, so I'm afraid to stop for fear of getting stuck. I have no choice but to keep going.

I could kick myself. If I'd been concentrating on my driving, I would be back at the community hall by now, instead of in the middle of nowhere. I have visions of running out of road, running out of gas, having my car tipped over by a bear, and spending the night upside down at the end of the world. To make matters worse, the sky is once more black with clouds, and it's spitting again. I add drowning to my list of worries.

I have just begun to consider putting the car into reverse and backing my way to the main road, when the trees give way to a field. The road isn't any wider here, but at least there's room to turn around. Before I can do that, though, I spot a truck about a hundred yards farther on. It's facing me. Curious, I keep driving.

As I get closer, I realize I've seen this truck before. It belongs to the weed whacker girl from the cemetery.

I pull around and park in front of the truck. Then I get out of my car, wander back to the old pickup, and peer inside. There are muddy boot prints on the floor mat, but no sign of the girl. I check out the bed of the truck. It contains a wooden plank, a shovel, a hoe, and a pitchfork, as well as a mound of something covered with a blue plastic tarpaulin. I lift a corner and look underneath.

Mud. Who puts mud in the back of their truck?

I squint out at the fields. On the north side of the road they're grassy and flat, but on other side they're hilly and dotted with bushes and trees.

I think about looking for the girl, but why? It's not like we're best buds. Far from it. And it's not as if she can tell me anything about Sam. He would have been gone long before she was even born. And even if she did know something, she's such a grouch, she would never tell me.

That's when it dawns on me that it's time to leave — not just the fields and this muddy road, but Farrow. The prospect catches me by surprise and makes me sad. Not just because I'm no closer to finding Sam than I was before I came, but because I'll sort of miss the place. In two short days, Farrow has grown on me. It has a laid-back feel that reminds me of Sam.

The people are characters, and in its own way the town is charming. The truth is I'll probably never be back, because if what everyone says is true, there will soon be no Farrow to come back to.

"Hey! Get away from that truck!"

I peer at the hilly field. The girl is staggering towards me behind a wheelbarrow piled with mud. When she reaches the road she lowers the barrow. She's puffing.

"What do *you* want?" she grumbles.

"Absolutely nothing," I say, stepping out of her way. "I took a wrong turn, and this is where it brought me. What are you doing here?"

She glares at me for a second before lowering the truck's tailgate and pulling back the tarp. "Did anybody ever tell you you're nosy?"

"Curious, not nosy."

"Same thing," she grunts and starts to shovel the mud into the truck."

"Why are you collecting mud?"

"Clay, not mud."

"Same thing."

She snorts and shakes her head. "Shows what you know."

A raindrop hits me on the top of the head, and I look up. "You better speed up your shovelling," I say. "It's starting to rain again, and I'd hate for your mud to get wet."

She doesn't answer, just keeps on shovelling. When she's finished, she pulls the tarp back in place, slides the plank out of the truck to make a ramp, and pushes the wheelbarrow up it. Then she returns the plank to the bed of the truck and hops into the cab.

It would appear our conversation is over, so I head back to my Honda. "Good talking to you. Have a nice day," I jibe as I pass her.

I start the car and switch on the windshield wipers. The rain is already coming down faster than they can sweep it away. Before pulling onto the road, I check my rear-view mirror to see the girl throw up the hood of her truck and stick her head inside.

Uh-oh. I put the car back into park, grab my umbrella, and head into the rain.

I join her under the hood. "Won't your truck start?"

She fiddles with some wires then climbs into the truck and turns the key. The motor chokes a couple of times, wheezes, and then dies. She turns the key a couple more times, but there's nothing. The girl gets out, slams the door, and then slams the hood down too.

"Damn battery's dead." She scowls at me like it's my fault.

"That's not good," I say.

"No kidding."

"So now what?"

Her tone is only slightly more civil as she asks, "Do you have jumper cables?"

"Considering I have no idea what jumper cables are, I couldn't tell you," I confess, "but we can look."

I pop the Honda's trunk and she roots around inside but comes up empty.

I gesture to my car. "I can give you a ride back to town."

She shakes her head. "I'll wait in my truck for the rain to stop."

I make a face. "And then what? Will the battery miraculously come to life again? Or were you planning to walk to town? If it rains much more, the road will be like quicksand."

She ignores me.

"You're just being stubborn," I tell her as I head back to my vehicle. "You don't have a choice, and you know it." I open the door and look back at her. "I'm leaving. So what's it going to be? Do you want a ride or not?"

Chapter Twelve

FOR FIVE MINUTES the only sounds are the rain, the windshield wipers, and the spin and spit of my tires churning up mud. The girl doesn't say a word, and neither do I. I'm too busy praying my little Honda doesn't get stuck. I have no idea what *she's* doing. Probably thinking up new gripes.

When we finally reach pavement again, I take a deep breath and pat the dash. "Good car." If it had bogged down in that mud, I don't know what I would've done.

The girl doesn't actually shift away from me, but she looks like she's thinking about it. "Do you always talk to your car?"

I remember asking Sam that same question about Lizzy. It's a memory I'm not willing to let the girl spoil, so I just shrug. "Where do you want me to drop you?"

"Anywhere near town," she says. "If you're staying at The Apple Tree, the corner of Fourth Avenue is fine."

I gesture to the world beyond the windshield. "In case you haven't noticed, it's peeing rain out there. You'll be drenched in thirty seconds. Just tell me where you want to go, and I'll take you."

She scowls as if I'm inconveniencing her instead of helping. "Randy's Service Station then."

I gawk at her. "There's a service station in Farrow?"

"Sort of. It used to be a service station. The pumps were taken out years ago, but Randy still has a hoist and his tow truck. He keeps extra cans of gas on hand for emergencies."

"Good to know," I say, filing the information away. "Where is this service station?"

"Main Street. The other end of Farrow."

"If you want, I could take you home. It's not a problem. Where do you live?"

She shakes her head. "I need my truck. Randy can get it."

"Tow trucks get stuck too," I say. "That road is getting really muddy."

"You haven't seen Randy's tow truck. And like I said, I need my vehicle."

"Why? What's so important that it can't wait until tomorrow?"

I feel her glaring at me. "Do you stick your nose into everybody's business, or am I the only lucky one?"

I take my eyes off the road long enough to glare back at her. "Actually, you *should* consider yourself lucky. If you talk to everyone like you do me, I'm surprised anybody bothers with you at all. Miss Congeniality you're not. In fact, I don't think I've ever met anyone with a bigger chip on her shoulder. It must be tough finding shirts to fit over it."

My sarcasm rolls right off her. "Har, har, har. Not only are you a busybody, you're a comedian too."

I slam on the brakes so hard, we both lurch towards the windshield.

"Hey!" she growls. "What's your problem?"

"What's yours?" I snarl back. "All I'm doing is making conversation. People do that, you know. Why do you have to make a federal case out of everything?"

I expect her to fire back with another smartass comment, but for once she doesn't say a word. Neither do I, and we spend the rest of the journey in silence.

When I see the red and white sign for Randy's Service, I feel like the Ancient Mariner about to dump the albatross. I pull up close to the building.

"Thanks," the girl says as she lets herself out of the car and runs for shelter. She couldn't sound less sincere if she tried.

"You're welcome," I mutter to her retreating back, but I don't mean it either. I don't even wait to see if anyone lets her in. I don't care.

As soon as I'm back on Main Street, my thoughts turn to Vancouver. It's time to go home. I gassed up my car on Friday, so aside from gathering my things at The Apple Tree, I'm all set. Vancouver is only a few hours from Merritt, so I could easily do the drive this evening. I consider it but then discard the idea. It's already been a full day, and I don't relish the thought of highway driving at night in the rain. Better to head out in the morning. Even if I have a leisurely breakfast with George, I can be home by early afternoon. I decide not to tell my mother. It'll be fun to surprise her. Besides, if she doesn't know I'm coming, she can't drive up to provide an escort.

Now that I've made the decision to leave Farrow, I start to get excited, though there's still a part of me that wants to stay. My gut just can't kick the feeling that the missing link to Sam's family — to *my* family — is in this town, and I can find it. All I need is more time.

"Let it go, Dani. It's wishful thinking," I scold myself and pull onto the grassy verge in front of The Apple Tree.

As I reach behind me for my backpack, I spy a pair of gloves on the passenger seat. They belong to the girl. "*Damn it!*" Why did she have to leave them behind? Now I have to hunt her down and return them. I feel my back go up. No, I don't. It's not my responsibility. She's the one who forgot them. What do I care? I'll just chuck them in the garbage. Problem solved. It's a nice thought but my over-developed conscience vetoes it. I scowl at the gloves one last time before getting out of my car. I'll drop them at the service station on my way out of town tomorrow. Maybe.

"George?" I call as I let myself into the cottage.

I turn toward the kitchen, expecting wonderful smells to be emanating from it. But there's nothing. The light isn't even on. The front door wasn't locked, so my landlady has to be here. "George?" I call again.

"In here," a voice replies. I follow it into the living room. Though the day is dark and dreary, there's no light on in there either. George is lying on the couch.

"I'm sorry," I say. "I didn't realize you were napping. I should have thought. After the bazaar, of course you're tired."

"Turn the light on, Dani." She gestures to a floor lamp across the room. "I wish it was just that. Yes, I'm tired, but that's not the issue. I'm afraid I've thrown my back out." She winces as she pushes herself up into a sitting position.

"Oh, no." I wince right along with her. "Is there anything I can do?"

She shakes her head. "It'll fix itself — eventually."

"What happened? Were you lifting something heavy?"

"No. Nothing like that. It was stupid, really. After I cleaned up my station at the bazaar and got everything put away at this end, I celebrated with a nice deep breath, which sent my back muscles into revolt." She starts to chuckle and then winces again. "They can't handle too much oxygen at one time anymore." She grins and immediately grimaces again. "They can't take a joke either." She uses the arm of the couch to help her stand.

I hurry over. "Do you need something? Just tell me. I'll get it."

George continues to struggle to her feet. "That's nice of you to offer, dear, but I need to pee, and I'm fairly certain you can't help me with that. Besides, I have to make supper."

"I *can* do that," I say, as I take her arm. "You're in a lot of pain, George. Maybe I should call a doctor."

She slaps my hand. "Stop fussing. I'll be fine. I already called my doctor. This back thing is nothing new. He's phoned a prescription into the pharmacy in Merritt. I'll pick it up tomorrow."

"I can pick it up for you right now," I say. "And you're not going to talk me out of it, George, so don't even try."

"I appreciate the thought, Dani, but you won't make it out of Farrow. When it rains, the dirt road leading to the highway becomes a quagmire. Unless your little car has four-wheel drive, you'll never get through."

Having just battled another of Farrow's mud roads, I know George is right.

"Okay," I concede. "But there's no way you can drive in your condition. I'll pick up your prescription first thing tomorrow. In the meantime, I'm making supper. You just take it easy." When she opens her mouth to protest, I add, "Save your breath. You're not the only one who can be stubborn."

———

Sunday morning is nothing but blue sky, making Saturday's deluge seem eons ago. It's unbelievably warm too, and I drink my coffee on George's front porch. When I've tidied up from breakfast and made George as comfortable as I can, I hop in my car and head off to the pharmacy in Merritt. I'm glad I didn't tell my mother I was coming home, since I'm clearly not — at least not until George is feeling better.

I'm a bit uneasy about venturing onto the muddy road, but most of yesterday's rain has either soaked in or run off, and aside from throwing mud all over the place (I wouldn't want to be a pedestrian) my little Honda rolls right along. In a single day it's gone from shiny silver to muck brown, but a good cleaning will fix that, so I resolve to spend the afternoon giving it a bath. The prospect lifts my spirits even more. It's a *nothing-can-go-wrong* kind of a day. Only good things can happen.

Maybe that's why I get sidetracked on the way back from Merritt. I've just turned off the highway and am squishing my way along the muddy road, window open, singing along with the radio, when I smell wood smoke. It reminds me of bonfires at Sam's trailer and I inhale deeply, suddenly wrapped in warm memories. Up ahead I see a plume of grey spiralling into the sky, and off to the right a narrow driveway twists into the leafless trees, leading to an old cabin. It's like being smacked in the face with a wet cloth. Something about that cabin says Sam. I don't know what, but there's something, and I can't ignore it.

Without stopping to think what I'm doing, I turn into the driveway. I have no idea who lives here, but people in Farrow are so friendly, I'm sure it'll be okay.

I'll ask about Sam. Who knows? I might even get some answers.

It isn't until I get almost to the cabin that I see the truck, and my spirits fall like a deflated soufflé. This must be where the girl lives.

Now all I want to do is leave. But as I go to put the car in reverse, I notice the gloves on the passenger seat. *Damn!* Growling under my breath, I switch off the car and grab the gloves. I shake them crossly. If the girl so much as looks at me funny, I'm going to swat her with them.

I march up to the log cabin, past terracotta pots filled with last year's shrivelled plants, a stone sun dial fringed with moss, and a rusty wagon wheel propped against a stack of firewood. Tattered cobwebs cling to the eaves and abandoned cocoons huddle in the chinks of the log walls. An old straw broom stands near the front door beside a jute mat with the greeting *Go Away*.

I'm tempted.

But I take a fortifying breath of spring air instead, and knock.

Chapter Thirteen

"ONE MISSISSIPPI, two Mississippi," I mutter. If I get to ten and the door hasn't opened, I'm dropping the gloves and leaving.

It cracks open on nine. With sleeves rolled up and muddy hands and arms held in front of her like a doctor preparing for surgery, the girl frowns at me. I mentally swat her with the gloves.

"You left these in my car," I say, holding them out.

Her frown dissolves. She hip checks the door open all the way and nods to a table inside. "Could you put them over there?" Then she grabs a rag that's already as muddy as her arms and attempts to clean herself.

I step inside. The cabin is a single room — a good size, though not huge, with sitting area, kitchen, bedroom, and some sort of workspace all rolled into one. The furniture is old, assorted discards from someone's attic by the look of it. Nothing matches. Still, a patchwork quilt, dried flowers, a bowl of potpourri, plump cushions, and a crackling fire in a pot-bellied stove give it a cozy feel. "Peer Gynt" is playing softly in the background. The cabin is way too pleasant and friendly to belong to this girl.

A shrill whistle pierces the air, shattering the mood. The girl removes a kettle from a hotplate and the whistling stops.

"I'm making tea," she says. "You can have some if you want."

It's not exactly a Martha Stewart invitation. In fact, it almost feels like the girl wants me to say no, but I'm not going to let her win at that game, so I tell her, "Sure," and shut the door. That's when I realize she and I don't even know each other's names. "By the way, I'm Dani Lancaster."

She nods and goes back to her tea-making.

"And you are —?"

She looks up again. "You mean my name?"

No, your age in dog years, I think sarcastically, but I don't so much as move my lips. I just nod.

"Alex," she replies. "Alex Burke."

I think of several things to say — all questions — but I don't ask them. She'll think I'm prying again. Thankfully, "Peer Gynt" fills the dead air.

"Do you take anything in your tea?" Alex says. "It's chai green."

"No. I'm good," I say as I join her at the small wooden table where she's placed our mugs.

The tea is scalding hot, but Alex drinks it without even flinching.

"How did you find me?" she asks.

"I was coming back from Merritt and saw the smoke." I shrug. "It looked inviting so I turned into the driveway. When I realized it was your place, I figured it was as good a time as any to return your gloves. I see you got your truck back."

She nods.

I glance at her dirty hands. "And your mud."

She rolls her eyes. "I told you — it's not mud. It's clay." She gestures to the work area behind her. "I'm a potter."

"Really?" A bell tinkles in my head, and I dig into my jacket pocket for the business card the girl at the bazaar gave me.

"Where'd you get that?" she asks when I pull it out.

"Alex Burke, Handcrafted Pottery," I read. It's followed by a website address and a cellphone number. I look up. "That's you?"

She takes another sip of her tea. "According to my birth certificate."

I strain to see over her shoulder into the work area. "I thought you were a guy. I mean, I thought Alex Burke was a guy. You made all that beautiful pottery at the bazaar?"

"You liked it?" She tries to sound cool and disinterested, but she can't completely hide her pleasure at the compliment.

"Are you kidding? It was fabulous! But it was all sold by the time I got there. That's why I picked up your card. I was hoping to buy some privately. Do you have any more pieces?" I'm still trying to see past her so she pushes herself away from the table and gestures for me to follow her.

"Not much right now. The bazaar more or less cleaned me out," she says, leading the way into the studio part of the cabin. "I'm working on some new stuff, but it won't be done for a few days. Are you looking for anything particular?"

"Not really. At the risk of giving you a swelled head, I pretty much loved everything I saw. My mom is an interior designer, and I wanted to buy some pieces for her."

Alex stops and turns back to me. She seems genuinely interested. "Really?"

"Yeah. So what do you have?"

Alex digs around in a cupboard and through some boxes and comes up with a bowl, a platter, a Japanese-style teapot, and a couple of mugs. Then she pulls a binder down from a shelf and flips it open. It's filled with photos of her work.

"These pieces are all I have on hand at the moment, but I have pictures of everything I've ever made — even the really bad stuff. Looking at those helps me remember where I started and how far I've come." She smiles self-consciously.

I pull out my phone. "May I take some pictures of your pictures? To show my mom."

She nods.

"And if these pieces are for sale, I'll take this one," I say, running a hand over the platter. I take photos of the pottery. "How much is it?"

She shakes her head. "No charge. You can have it."

"No way," I protest. "I know what you were selling your stuff for at the bazaar, and I also know that's cheap compared to what they would retail for in Vancouver stores. You can't give this away."

"Consider it my way of apologizing," she says.

"Apologizing? For what?"

She rolls her eyes. "How about for being a major bitch. I know how I've acted. I've been totally rude and nasty to you since the first time we met."

I shrug. "True." Then I add hastily, "But that doesn't mean you have to give your pottery away. A simple *I'm sorry* would work too."

"I *am* sorry. Really. I know it's hard to believe, but I'm not usually so snarky. It's just that my dad dropped a bomb on me the day I talked to you at the cemetery, and I was in panic mode." She shrugs. "So I took it out on you."

"Is everything okay now?"

She wanders back to the table and throws herself into her chair. "It's not the end of the world or anything like that," she says. "Well, not exactly, though it feels like it."

I sit down across from her and sip my tea.

"Until last June, I lived in Merritt with my parents. Then out of the blue, my dad and mom decided to pick up and move to Ontario. My dad got offered some big promotion and he took it. Fine for them, but I've lived my whole life in Merritt. I didn't want to leave. I wanted to stay right where I've always been and do my pottery." She sighs. "Well, that idea went over like a lead balloon. My father has no use for artsy-fartsy stuff, as he calls it. He wants me to go to university and become a teacher or lawyer or accountant — something with a degree and a regular salary. Ever since I graduated from high school last year, it's been an ongoing war between us. If it weren't for my mom, we probably would've killed each other by now. I don't know how she managed it, but somehow she convinced my dad to let me stay. She even talked him into giving me a monthly allowance — not much, but enough to pay for my food and other basics." She holds her hands out to take in the room. "The cabin belongs to my grandparents. It's been in the family forever, and they let me stay in it rent-free. The truck I bought dirt cheap. It's not much, but it gets me from here to there and gives me a way to get clay and to transport my pottery. It's a pretty bare-bones existence, but I'm okay with it."

I regard her over the top of my mug. "But —"

She sighs again. "But on Thursday morning my dad called to say that as of June 1st, he's cutting off my allowance. If I agree to go to university in Toronto, he'll pay my way east and even cover the cost of my classes, but if I decide to stay in B.C., I'm on my own. *Pa-dum-pum!* Talk about having the rug pulled out from under me. I'm not making a lot of money from my pottery — still not self-sufficient, but things are definitely moving in the right direction. Without my parents' support, though, there's no way I can continue."

"So what are you going to do?"

"I don't know yet. But I'll figure something out."
She points to my mug. "More tea?"

"Sure," I say. "Thanks."

She grabs both mugs and heads over to the counter. "So what brings you to Farrow?"

"I'm trying to find my father. Well, not him exactly. He's dead. I'm trying to track down his roots. I want to know where I came from. But it's tough. My dad was left on the doorstep of John and Hannah Swan when he was just a few days old. He never knew who his birth parents were. I came here hoping I could find out."

"Any luck?"

"No. It's just been one dead end after another."

"So are you giving up?"

Her words catch me by surprise. They're almost like an accusation or a dare. The truth is I *was* giving up. If George hadn't hurt her back, I'd be on my way to Vancouver this very minute. But she did hurt her back, and that made me stay. Then I was pulled into Alex's driveway by nothing more than woodsmoke. Maybe it's just serendipity, but it looks like I'm not finished in Farrow after all.

With renewed determination, I shake my head. "Giving up? No. Are you?"

She doesn't answer, but I didn't expect her to. I change the subject.

"You're lucky to live in Farrow. Small towns are great. The people are friendly. The pace is slower. There's actually time to smell the roses."

"Pretty soon all there'll be is roses," Alex snorts. "Farrow is on its last legs. People don't want to leave, but they have no choice. There are lots of craftspeople here. You saw what it was like at the bazaar. So many talented artisans. But without a bigger population or at least steady traffic through the town, there's no way for them to sell their wares. They've toughed it out as long as they can. It's time to go."

"But that just seems so wrong. What would make them stay?"

"Services, for one thing, like decent roads and clean water. And industry. People need jobs. When Farrow started out, it had mining and the railroad. But those are long gone. What industry is going to move into Farrow now?"

Without warning, Alex's words ignite a fuse in my head, and my brain suddenly explodes like a fireworks display with ideas shooting in every direction.

Chapter Fourteen

MY HEAD IS BUZZING like a bee's nest. Alex has stirred up so many ideas, I don't know which one to act on first. All I know is that if I can convert my brain waves into actual plans, I might have the answers to a lot of people's problems. As soon as I get back to The Apple Tree and give George her medicine, I hole up in my bedroom to make some phone calls.

First my mother.

"Hey, Mom," I say when she picks up, "did you get the photos I sent you?"

"On my phone?"

"Yes." Obviously my mother hasn't checked her messages. "I sent them a few minutes ago."

"I was talking with a client. As soon as I hung up, you called. I haven't had a chance to check for messages."

"Do it now. Please," I add before she can get on my case for being pushy or rude — maybe both. "Then call me back. This is important."

I end the call before she can protest. If she wants to give me heck, she'll have to return my call.

After two minutes, my phone is still quiet. I stare at it hard, willing it to ring. When it does, I pick up before it's even finished its first chime.

"Well?" I blurt anxiously.

"Yes, I am well. Thanks for asking, Dani."

"Mother!" I fume. "Don't be funny. What did you think of the pictures? Isn't the pottery fabulous?"

She laughs. "Good Lord, Dani. I can't remember the last time you were this excited. What's gotten into you? Does this have something to do with Sam?"

That takes a bit of the wind out of my sails. It also surprises me a little. I *am* excited, but it *isn't* about Sam. In fact, for the last hour I haven't thought about Sam at all. A wave of guilt washes over me, but I can't let it douse my fire, so I push it from my mind. "No. It doesn't. Every lead I've followed has fizzled out — so far. That doesn't mean I'm giving up, though," I add hastily. "I'm sure somebody around here knows something. I just haven't found that person yet.

"That's not why I called," I say, steering the conversation back on track. "What do you think of the pottery?"

"It's beautiful," Mom says. "Truly. Who's the artist?"

Though my mother can't see me, I smile. "I knew

you'd like it. That's why I got you a piece — the platter."

Mom gasps. "Oh, Dani, thank you, but it must have cost a small fortune!"

"You're worth it," I tease. "Actually it was free, though I did try to pay. The artist wouldn't take my money."

"Why on earth not?"

"It's a long story, but let's just say she gave me a pretty hard time my first few days in Farrow, and the platter was her way of apologizing."

"Wow. That's some apology. It's a gorgeous piece. As are the others you sent pictures of. Such a unique style. Strange I haven't seen any of your friend's work in Vancouver. Anywhere, for that matter. What is her name?"

"Alex Burke. She's young, Mom. A year older than me. She's only been selling her stuff for a few months, and as you can imagine, there's not much of a market in Farrow."

I've reached the tricky part of the conversation. I lick my lips before wading in. "She's so talented, Mom."

"I can see that."

"I thought her work was exactly the sort of thing you use in your designs."

"It is, most definitely. If you're hinting that you'd like me to buy more of her work, you can relax. I'd be happy to. The girl has talent."

I breathe a little easier. One obstacle down; one to go. "That's great. Thanks. Alex will be so thrilled." I clear my throat before continuing. "I was thinking." I pause, trying to decide how best to couch my words.

"Uh-oh," Mom says. "I always get a little nervous when you start thinking."

Since I can't back out now, I steamroll ahead. "Well, I was wondering ... you said yourself you haven't seen anything like Alex's pottery anywhere in Vancouver ... so I thought maybe ... you know because you have so many connections ... well, I thought if you showed some of the retailers her work ... I'm not asking you to become her agent or anything ... but —"

Mom laughs for the second time during the conversation. "For goodness sake, Dani, finish a sentence. What you're not saying is you want me to see if I can find some outlets for Alex's work."

I heave a huge sigh. "Yes. She only has until June to become self-sufficient. After that her father cuts off her allowance, and she'll be forced to give up her art and go to university. Do you really think she can make a living at this?"

"I know so. Eventually, I'm going to need actual samples of the product, but in the meantime, send as many photos as you can, and I'll see what I can do."

I give her Alex's website address. "Thanks," I say. "You're a lifesaver, Mom."

"Hey, I said I'd ask around. Don't go popping the cork on the champagne just yet. Wait until I've made some inquiries. It may take a few days."

"I know you'll come through," I say again.

"You're the best, Mom. I love you. Now could you put Reed on?"

"What?" she squeaks. "Talk about the bum's rush. Good thing I love you too. Hang on." And though she covers up the phone, I hear her yell for Reed.

"Hey, Dani," he says as soon as he takes the phone, and I can't help wondering if my mother is right beside him, listening in. "How's it going?"

"Good, Reed." I know I should make small talk, but I'm too excited. I zoom right to the point. "Have you found a site yet for your new brewery redistribution centre?"

He chuckles, just like my mother did. Obviously I'm pretty darn amusing this morning. "No," he says, and though he's stopped laughing, I can tell he's still smiling. "But I'm guessing *you* have."

I know he's teasing me, but I don't care. "As a matter of fact, I think I might have. You said you want it to be in a small town, right?"

"Right."

"But near a main highway."

"Yup."

"In the Okanagan."

"Right again."

"You're looking to hire local people?"

"Might as well give them the work as anyone."

"Then I think I have just the place. Farrow."

"That little town you're in right now?"

"Yes. There's a perfect location here for your plant. The government took over some property for unpaid taxes, so you could probably get it dirt cheap. You'd have to pave a couple of miles of road, but you told me you'd probably have to upgrade roads anyway, since they can't always stand up to truck traffic."

"That's true."

"I don't know anything about zoning, building codes, government bureaucracy, or any of that stuff, but I really think you should take a look at this place, Reed. It has potential. The population has been dwindling since the mining companies and railroad pulled out, because there's no industry. The distribution centre could be that industry. It could be the answer for you *and* Farrow. And if your company is bringing work and money into the area, people would stay, and the government would have to provide more amenities. Wouldn't it?"

That makes him laugh again. "Possibly, but don't go getting ahead of yourself. I haven't seen anything else I like so far, so it doesn't hurt to take a look at Farrow. But don't go getting your hopes up. I'll check out the logistics of the town, and if there's a possibility of working something out, I'll come up and see the place. Give me a couple of days. I can come up there on Wednesday. Hang on a second, Dani." I can hear my mother in the background, and then Reed's back on the line. "Correction. My social director — aka your mother — informs me *we* can come up on Wednesday. She says she'll have some answers for you then about whatever it is you were talking to her about, and I can take a look around Farrow. That gives you a few more days to continue your search for Sam. Then we can all drive back to Vancouver together."

I don't want to commit to that last part. Not yet. But I don't want to risk jeopardizing the headway I've made this morning either, so I don't baulk. I simply say I'll phone before he and Mom leave Vancouver, and I'll see them on Wednesday.

One more call to make. This one's a long shot, but I'm on a roll, and neither Farrow nor I have anything to lose. But Sam's old friend might have something to gain — and give.

"Hello, Arlo. It's Dani Lancaster. How are you?"

"Dani! Hey yourself. I wasn't expecting to hear from you quite so soon. I can't tell you how much I enjoyed our little talk the other day. Sam has been on my mind ever since. I thought of a bunch more stories. Maybe we can get together again one of these days and I can tell them to you over another cup of coffee.

"How about Tuesday?" I say. "That's your day off, right?"

He sputters for a few seconds. I've clearly caught him off guard. "Are you coming back to Barriere?" he finally asks.

"Actually, I was hoping you might come to Farrow," I say. "That's the town Sam was left in as a baby. That's where I am now. You could take the bus to Merritt — I'll pay, of course — and I'll pick you up there and bring you to Farrow. You might need more than one day, though," I tell him. "If you can't get another day off work with pay, I can cover your wages too. This is kind of important."

"What are you talking about, girl? You're not making any sense. Does this have something to do with Sam?"

I smile. "Actually, yes. It does. Arlo, do you remember how you said you regretted that you would never be able to pay Sam back for helping you when you were down, and I said you could pay it forward?"

"Uh-huh," he replies warily.

"Well, I think I have a way for you to do that. I have a proposition. Farrow is an amazing little town, but it's dying. It has lots of potential, but it's not being tapped. It needs somebody to organize things. What I'm hoping is that you'll be that somebody. I would like to hire you as a consultant."

"A consultant?" He seems truly surprised. "I'm an over-the-hill rodeo cowboy, not a consultant. You're barkin' up the wrong tree here, Dani."

"I don't think so," I say. "I know you're not trained or anything, but I have a feeling you might just be what this little town needs. You know people, and the success you've had with the rodeo in Barriere proves you have organizational skills."

"What would you be wanting me to do?"

"Well, a few things, actually. There are many gifted artisans in this town, but they aren't organized and they don't know about marketing. I thought maybe you could help them set up a guild, so that they can work together and learn how to make a living at what they do. That would include organizing a spring and fall fair to showcase their wares. It would need to draw people from all over B.C. — even farther if that's possible! That can't be that different than putting on a rodeo, can it? And finally, I'd like you to help the locals organize an annual rodeo, like you do in Barriere. There used to be one here in Farrow, so there is a venue, but that was a long time ago, and it needs work."

I take a deep breath before continuing. "I know this is asking a ton, but it would be the perfect way to pay Sam back. This was his town. You don't have to give me your answer right away. I know you need to think about it. All I'm asking for now is that you come and check the place out."

"One question. If Farrow is dying, where's the money coming from to pay for this?"

There's no point in lying, so I say, "Sam left me an inheritance. I think he'd like to see it used to save his town."

Arlo chuckles. It is clearly my day to tickle people's funny bones.

"What are you laughing at?"

"I was just thinking that the apple doesn't fall far from the tree."

Chapter Fifteen

WHEN I GET OFF THE PHONE with Arlo, I'm flying high. If everything works out, Alex's pottery business is going to take off and she won't have to move to Ontario, Reed will create much-needed jobs for Farrow residents by relocating part of his brewery operation, and Arlo will organize the locals so that the town's personality has a way to shine.

Though George insists she's feeling much better, I make lunch.

As she blows on her soup, she eyes me suspiciously. "What are you grinning at, girl? You look like the cat that swallowed the canary."

I sigh happily. "It's spring. I love spring."

"Hogwash," she snorts. "That is not a *gay-as-the-buds-of-May* smile you're wearing. It's a *you're-up-to-something* leer. You're up to your eyebrows in a plot, or my name's not George Washington."

I shrug and change the subject. "Do you have a bucket and rag I can use, George? And a hose? I thought I'd wash my car this afternoon. It got pretty dirty yesterday."

She nods.

"Great." Then I remember about Arlo coming. "Also, do you have another room you can let for one night? Someone I know is coming to Farrow, and he'll need a place to stay."

She wags her finger at me. "I don't tolerate any funny business in this house."

I choke on my soup. When I stop coughing, I gape at George. "Arlo isn't my boyfriend!"

"Arlo, is it?" she harrumphs. "And who might he be when he's out, and why is he coming to Farrow?"

"He's a friend of my father's. And he's coming to Farrow to talk to me about Sam." There's no point in telling George the real reason I asked Arlo to come. And anyway, I'm not really lying. I'm sure Arlo and I *will* talk about Sam. "You're awfully inquisitive."

"Just doing a background check. I'm an old woman. I can't be too careful about who I take in. Axe murderers can make a big mess."

Of course that makes me laugh. I shake my head. "Do you have any idea how ornery you get when you're not feeling well?"

She scowls at me over her soup spoon. "Nonsense and horse feathers. I'm feeling just fine."

"Then it's okay for Arlo to stay here?"

"Hmmph," she mumbles.

I take that as a yes. "It will just be the one night," I assure her. "And when he leaves, I'll change the bedding, so you don't have to worry about putting your back out again. By the way, my mom and stepdad are coming up from Vancouver on Wednesday."

"You're just a regular little social butterfly, aren't you?" she says. "Are they staying here too?"

"Well, that depends on you," I tell her. "If it's going to be too much work for you, I'm sure they'll be fine with getting a motel in Merritt."

She waves away my words. "Don't be ridiculous. I told you I'm fine. Besides, I'm sure your mother and I will have a lot to talk about."

I have no idea what that's supposed to mean, and I don't ask.

———

I slosh warm, soapy water onto my Honda and start to scrub. The bubbly white suds quickly turn muddy. I hose them away and watch as a tiny river of dirty water trickles down the road and slithers off the pavement into the grassy verge. When I'm done, water droplets bead on my car and sparkle in the sun like a million miniature prisms.

I step back to admire my work. A passing motorist honks and gives me a thumbs-up. I smile and wave. Already I feel a part of this place.

After putting away the car-washing supplies, I head to my room. I peel off my dirty shirt and reach blindly into my suitcase for a fresh one. My hand touches something hard, smooth, and cold. It's the framed photo of Sam that the Sheffields gave me. The sight of it reminds me that I haven't achieved what I came here to do, and a little of the sunshine leaks out of the day.

Picking up the photo, I drop onto the bed. I stare at Sam, and he stares back. *Well?* his eyes say. I sigh and look away. Well, indeed. Since I started this journey to find the missing pieces of my father's life, I've learned a lot about Sam, the person, but nothing about his parents and the rest of his family.

The rest of *my* family. I have to keep reminding myself that it's my family too. For seventeen years I knew who I was — at least who *I* thought I was, but I took my identity — my ancestry — for granted. It just *was*, like my hair colour and my shoe size. Then suddenly half of my family tree gets ripped away and there's a gaping hole in my life. Half of me is missing. Maybe it shouldn't bother me, but it does. I need to know where I came from in order to understand who I am.

But it's like peering into a black cave. I know there's something in there, but all I see is darkness.

I set the photo on the night table and rummage through my backpack for the half-heart necklace. It's cold, like the clue it provides. I run my finger over the rough edge where it's been cut. Why would someone do that? To share the heart, for sure — but why? And with whom? Did Sam's mother give him half and keep half, as a way of staying connected to him?

It bothers me that I don't know, and even more that I may never know. There are so many things I might never find out. And the really awful part is that I could grow old and die without ever getting any answers. In three days my mom and Reed will be here, and when they leave, I'll be leaving with them. There is no way my mother will go back to Vancouver without me, and that means the end of my search for Sam.

I slip the chain around my neck and tuck the heart inside my shirt. Then I flop onto my back and stare at the ceiling. How did the day go from exhilarating to depressing in just a few minutes?

This morning everything was roses. I was so sure all my little schemes were going to work out. Alex was going to make a go of her pottery business, Reed was going to set up his distribution centre in Farrow, and Arlo was going to promote the town's culture. What the heck was I thinking? I'm eighteen years old, for goodness sake — how can I still believe in fairy tales? Nothing turns out happily ever after. Especially not the kind of stuff I'm trying to pull off. Save a town! Piece of cake. Send an artist to the top! No problem.

I think Alex is an amazing potter, but it takes more than talent to make a business fly. I've seen how hard my mom works at her designing business. Reed too, with his brewery. There's no way I could do all the stuff they do, and yet I'm still naïve enough to think that all Alex needs to succeed is a few marketing connections. And what if Mom can't generate interest in Alex's work? All she has are a few photos. She doesn't even have any actual pieces of pottery to show people.

And what about Arlo? He's a really nice guy, and though he may have experience helping with the Barriere rodeo, he's no urban planner. I'm bringing him to Farrow on a hunch — a gut feeling. But what does he actually know about planning a community fair or organizing a guild? I was counting on him to help showcase Farrow's personality, but what if he can't?

I cringe when I think of my proposal to Reed. Yes, he is looking to relocate his distribution centre, and he did say he wanted somewhere away from a city, but Farrow might be just a little *too* far away. What if Farrow doesn't meet the needs of the brewery at all? What if Reed takes one look at the place and thinks I brought him here on a wild goose chase? He'll never trust me again.

I feel sick. I thought I was helping everyone, but what if all I'm really doing is poking my nose where it doesn't belong? Maybe Alex was right about that. I might be making things worse instead of better. If things go sideways, the residents of Farrow could chase me out of town. And Reed will be right there, cheering them on.

"Aren't you Doctor Jekyll and Mr. Hyde today," George says at dinner.

I frown. "What are you talking about?"

"Well, at lunch time you were grinning like a Cheshire cat, and now you look like you might throttle someone. Even when I was going through the change, I never had mood swings that big. But since you wouldn't tell me what had you walking on air at lunchtime, I doubt you'll tell me what's got your knickers in a twist now."

"I'm fine," I grumble.

George turns back to her supper. "That's what I thought."

Chapter Sixteen

IT'S A LONG NIGHT. I spend most of it arguing with myself and seeing how tangled I can get in the bedding. By six o'clock I'm punch-drunk tired, but I still can't sleep. I throw off the covers and drag myself out of bed. My head is thick, my body aches, and my eyes feel like I removed my mascara with battery acid. I dress quietly and tiptoe to the kitchen. Hopefully a cup of tea will help.

And there's George at the table with a hot water bottle propped between her back and the spindles of the chair.

"The kettle's still hot," she says.

I rummage through the cupboard for a mug. "Your back still bothering you?" I take my tea and slide onto a chair across from her.

"Mostly just stiff. Rigor mortis sets in during the

night. Dress rehearsal for the real thing, most likely. One of these mornings I'm gonna wake up dead." She allows herself a chuckle before adding, "And what's *your* problem?"

"Couldn't sleep."

"I can see that. No card-carrying teenager I've ever known would voluntarily open an eye before ten o'clock, let alone actually get out of bed. So what was keeping you awake?"

I shrug. "My brain. It was one of those nights I couldn't seem to switch it off."

"Sounds to me like you've got too much going on in there. Best way to fix that is to get rid of some of it."

I snort. "Right. And exactly how do I do that?"

"You deal with it."

———

After breakfast, I put on my sweats and go for a run — to Alex's cabin. I'm trying to jolt my body back to life and blow the cobwebs out of my head, but I'm also trying to follow George's advice.

I knock.

"It's open!" Alex hollers from somewhere inside.

I let myself in. Alex is unloading her kiln, so I make my way to the back of the cabin. When I see the new pottery, I gasp. "Alex, this is gorgeous! But it's different than your other stuff."

She shrugs. "I was experimenting with a new glaze. You like it?"

"Oh, yeah. It's very earthy or rustic or — I don't know — but it's something. Something spectacular! You're amazing."

"Thanks." She smiles. "Now all I have to do is sell it."

"Actually, I wanted to talk to you about that," I say. "Can we sit down?"

"Sure." She gestures to the couch.

I flop down, hug a cushion, and get straight to the point. "My mom is going to buy some of your work. I don't know how much, but she really likes your pottery and she thinks she can use it in her designs. Chances are she might become a regular customer."

Alex's face turns into one huge grin. "That's great. Dani, thank you so much for sending her the pictures. This is wonderful news!"

I nod and smile. "I thought you'd be pleased." I pause. "There's more."

Alex stops smiling. "What else?"

"Well, I wasn't going to say anything until it was for sure, but last night I started having an ulcer thinking about how you might react, so I figured I better tell you now."

"What is there for me to react to?"

"Nothing. But considering how you've accused me of not minding my own business a few times, I got worried that you might interpret what I've done as interfering in your life again — and that is so not what I'm trying to do."

"Okay, now you're starting to scare me. What have you done?"

"Nothing bad. Honest. I told you my mom is an interior designer."

She nods.

"Well, because of her business, she has connections in the decorating world — wholesalers, retailers, those kinds of people. So, I sort of asked her to see if any of them would be interested in selling your work."

I cringe, waiting for her to blow up.

"And?"

I ungrimace. "And you're not mad?"

"Of course I'm not mad. This is a good thing. You're trying to help me."

"Yeah, but without your knowledge or permission."

She laughs. "You sound disappointed. Do you *want* me to freak out?"

"No. I just thought —"

"Has your mom had any luck?"

"It's too soon to tell. I only talked to her about it yesterday. But my mother isn't a lady to waste time. I expect to hear some news one way or another in a couple of days." I don't mention that my mother is coming to Farrow, and Alex can talk to her herself. There's no point getting her hopes up more than they already are.

And they are definitely up. Alex is positively glowing.

"This is fantastic!" She hugs herself. "This might be exactly what I need to keep me afloat."

Though that is my thought too, I don't want her getting airborne, so I say, "Don't go counting your chickens before they're hatched. At this point it's just a possibility. That's all."

She takes a calming breath, though it doesn't appear to help. "Maybe so," she says, "but it's one more possibility than I had ten minutes ago."

————

Since Alex has taken my promotional efforts on her behalf so positively, I tell her about my plan to bring Arlo to Farrow. To my surprise, she thinks it's a good idea and even volunteers to help show him around and field questions I probably don't know the answers to.

So after I pick him up at the bus station in Merritt the next morning, I swing by Alex's cabin.

"Nice work," Arlo murmurs as he checks out Alex's pottery. "I'm no expert on this sort of thing, but even I can tell this is mighty fine craftsmanship."

"Thank you." Alex beams. "Now if I could just figure out how to make it earn me a living."

"I understand a lot of folks around here have that problem," Arlo says.

"Well, there's not really a marketplace here," she replies. "Except for the spring bazaar, there are no outlets in Farrow at all. There used to be stores, but they've shut down. Shopkeepers have either moved away or taken jobs in Merritt or some other town they can commute to. The buildings are all here. It wouldn't be hard to open them up again, but without customers there's no point. If we craftspeople want to sell our stuff, we have to find a store somewhere else.

Plus, we have to get our stuff there. Mostly places will only take a few pieces at a time, and though it's on consignment, we still have to pay the store a big chunk of change. Between the travel and the cost of materials, it's hard to earn any money without charging huge prices, and nobody wants to do that. That's why the spring bazaar is so good. I sold everything I had. I wish I'd had more, because I could've sold that too."

"How many of you artisans are there in Farrow?" Arlo asks.

Alex thinks a minute. "Here and over Brookmere way and thereabouts, there must be around fifty, I'd say."

"And what sorts of things do they make?"

"Everything!" she exclaims and starts counting on her fingers. "Wood carvings, bronze castings, stone sculptures, paintings, blown glass, jewellery, quilts."

"Leaded glass, knitting and crocheting, woodcuts, weaving," I add when Alex pauses for air.

"Photography, etching, leatherwork, paper ..."

We tag-team our way through a dozen more crafts before Arlo stops us.

"That's quite a list."

"And we're not just talking casual crafters, either," I point out. "I've seen the products these people turn out. This is high-quality merchandise. And," I add, "compared to what they'd sell for in Vancouver, the goods are way underpriced."

"Sounds like you craftspeople could definitely do better if you pulled together. Aside from the bazaar, has anybody every tried joining forces?" Arlo says.

Alex shrugs. "I don't think so. Not that I know of, anyway."

"Instead of everybody reinventing the wheel for themselves and shouldering all the costs, you could pool your resources. You could share shipping. You could rent a shop and take turns manning it. You could do some research about prices. You could become online vendors. I haven't had a chance to speak with any guilds yet, but I will. I'm betting there are all kinds of ways you could make things work."

I feel myself smiling. Maybe I was right about Arlo after all.

"Now tell me about this here Farrow rodeo. I'm gonna like sinking my teeth into that one."

"Fergie would be the one to tell you about that," Alex says. "The rodeo was already history by the time I started spending time in Farrow."

"Who's Fergie?" I say.

But before Alex can answer, Arlo cuts in. "Fergie? Not Fergie Witter, by any chance?"

Alex's jaw drops open. "You know Fergie?"

Arlo grins. "If we're talkin' rodeo, I sure do. Fergie was a big name on the circuit when I started out. So this is where he settled then? Well, I'll be go to hell."

———

I guess you can take the cowboy out of the rodeo, but you can't take the rodeo out of the cowboy. As soon as we hunt Fergie Witter down, it's like old home week for him and Arlo. The two men hadn't known each other well on the circuit — one was just starting in the business as the other was finishing up — but they knew the same people, and the fact that they both have rodeo in their blood bonds them as nothing else can.

Once the memories and stories are out of the way, Arlo gets down to business.

"So, what say you show me the old rodeo grounds you have here and tell me how it was back in the day?"

"You betcha," Fergie grins, and we drive over to the community hall. "It weren't a huge rodeo, you understand," he says as he shows us around the corral. "But it was respectable. It drew the local cowboys as well as the ones on their way up to or down from the circuit."

"No grandstand," Arlo says.

"There used to be," Fergie says. "It got tore down when the wood started to rot. It was an accident waitin' to happen. Same with the barn."

"What kind of a turnout did you get?" Arlo asks.

"In its glory years, the stands were full for the whole three days, so probably ten thousand people, I'd say."

Arlo nods toward the community hall. "Did you hold a dance too?"

Fergie spits into the dirt and spreads his arms. "Dance, cookout, hayride, the whole shebang. We did it up right. I can show you. There's a photo album in the hall. C'mon."

We tromp back to the community hall and Fergie unlocks the door.

"What's the point of locking the place up when half the town has a key?" I whisper to Alex. All I get in answer is an elbow to the ribs.

"Oh, yeah, those were the days," Fergie sighs when we've looked at the old rodeo photos. "It takes me back." Then he squints at Arlo. "I'd give my favourite cowboy boots to see the rodeo up and running again, but it would be a foolhardy thing to attempt. It would never fly. This place is dying. Why are you even thinking about it?"

Arlo smiles. "Thinking doesn't cost a body anything but time, and you just never know what the result will be." But when we've dropped Fergie back at his house and are back at Alex's cabin, Arlo says, "Fergie has a point, Dani. And no offence to you, Alex, cuz you live here and all, but Farrow is well on its way to becoming a ghost town. Trying to put on a rodeo where there aren't any people to see it is plain foolishness. *Expensive* foolishness. I know you mean well, Dani, but I don't see how this can work."

I glance at Arlo and Alex. He looks grim and she looks apologetic.

"So that's your only reservation about going ahead with this?" I say. "The shortage of people in Farrow?"

"You have to admit that's a pretty big problem," Alex points out.

"It might be," I say.

"*Might* be? Are you serious?" she blurts. "How can y —"

I hold up my hand. "Before you have a hissy fit,

hear me out. I may have a way to turn things around here. Farrow is dying, because there is no industry — no jobs. Right?"

They both nod.

"Well, it just so happens that my stepdad owns a very large brewery, and he's looking to open a new distribution facility somewhere in the Okanagan. From what I know of his requirements, Farrow could fill the bill. And if the distribution centre went in, it would provide industry and jobs, which means people could come back here. The town could start growing again."

Alex is gaping at me. "Is this a for-sure thing?"

I shake my head. "No, but my stepdad is coming to see the place. He likes what I've told him, and the next step is to see if it's a feasible move."

"When's he coming?"

"He and my mom will be here tomorrow."

Chapter Seventeen

THAT EVENING MY MOM CALLS with good news. Even without seeing the merchandise, two distributors have expressed an interest in carrying Alex's pottery. Mom says they can tell from the photographs that the pieces are excellent quality and the unique style will have customer appeal. Once Mom gets her hands on some actual pieces, she is confident she can convince even more vendors to take on Alex's work.

Mom says she and Reed should make it to Farrow by early afternoon. That gives me time to get Arlo back on the bus to Barriere before they arrive. I'd be lying if I said I wasn't nervous. Everything rides on Reed moving the brewery's distribution facility to Farrow, and at this point there's no telling which way that's going to go. Reed may see the town's potential, like I do, or he may decide it doesn't have what it takes. I just don't know.

———

I drop Arlo at the bus station and pick up a couple of subs before heading back to Farrow. As soon as I turn off the highway, I see the smoke curling into the sky above Alex's cabin, and suddenly I can't get there fast enough. She is going to be thrilled when I tell her about the headway my mother has made.

I don't waste any time sharing the news, and just as I expect, Alex is pumped. She can't even sit down to eat her sandwich, which means I spend the whole time pivoting on my chair, trying to keep her in sight. Her nervous energy is contagious and I find myself getting wound as tight as a spring right along with her. In self-defence, I finally get up to leave.

"I'm sure my mom will want to talk to you," I say as I head for the door. "I'll call you when they get here."

Alex nods so hard, it's a wonder her head doesn't snap off and roll across the room. She stuffs her cellphone into her jeans. She's practically bouncing. "I'll be waiting for your call."

I roll my eyes. "For God's sake, Alex, calm down."

"How can I? I'm too excited. This could be the break I need."

"Maybe," I say. "I hope so, but don't get your heart set on it. We'll know better once we talk to my mom. In the meantime, you need something to take your mind off this. Listen to some music. Go throw some clay. Run a marathon! I don't know. There must be something that will distract you."

She grins. "How about Chris Hemsworth? I'm pretty sure he could hold my attention."

———

I might have been the voice of reason while I was talking to Alex, but the truth is I am just as anxious as she is. In fact, it's a miracle I don't wear out George's living room rug waiting for Mom and Reed to arrive. When the BMW finally pulls up behind my Honda, I want to run outside, yipping like a little kid. But I don't. Somehow I manage to contain my excitement and stroll down the path like an honest-to-goodness, pulled-together adult, and I start to think maybe I should pursue a career in acting.

It's Mom who loses it. "Oh, Dani!" she gushes the second she sees me, throwing her arms around me and squeezing so hard I can't breathe for a second.

I laugh and hug her back. "Good grief, Mom. It hasn't even been two weeks. You'd think I'd been away for two years."

On his way to the trunk, Reed kisses the top of my head. "It's good to see you, kiddo." Then he says to my mother, "You see, Joanna? I told you she'd be fine."

Reluctantly, she lets me go. "So I worry. What's wrong with that? It's a mother's prerogative."

"Let me help you with the bags, Reed," I say.

He waves me away. "I've got it. We didn't bring much. You show your mom the B&B."

Mom and I lock arms and start up the path.

"This is really lovely," she says, taking in the yard and cottage. "I bet it's stunning when everything is in bloom."

"Probably," I agree. I lead her inside. "Let me introduce you to George Washington."

She pulls back. "I beg your pardon."

I laugh and drag her toward the kitchen and its mouth-watering aromas. George has been cooking all day.

"George, I'd like you to meet my mother, Joanna Malcolm. Mom, this is George Washington, the proprietor of this fine establishment."

"George?" My mother extends her hand.

"Georgina." George grins. "But nobody calls me that. Pleased to meet you."

"What a lovely cottage you have," Mom says. "So charming and cosy. No wonder Dani has stayed so long."

"Are you saying I've worn out my welcome?"

"Nonsense," George jumps in before my mother can reply. "Dani and I get along like a house on fire. She's more like family than a paying guest."

"But I *am* paying," I throw in quickly when my mother raises an eyebrow in my direction.

"Hello?" Reed calls from the front hall. "Anybody home?"

"In the kitchen," I holler. "Follow the scrumptious smells."

"Have you had lunch?" George asks my mother.

"Hey, I thought you didn't provide lunch," I cut in.

George shrugs. "It's my bed and breakfast. I can change the rules if I want."

We all laugh just as Reed walks in.

"Now that could give a guy a complex." He grins.

Mom pulls him forward. "George, I'd like you to meet my husband, Reed. Reed, this is our hostess, George Washington." When he cocks his head in surprise, she adds, "It's the truth."

The three of them snicker.

I roll my eyes. Same old joke.

"Dani," George says, "why don't you show your folks to their room and I'll make us a pot of tea."

"Right," I nod. "Follow me. We have put you in the east wing in a lovely room with a view. I hope you find your accommodations to your liking. Enjoy your stay, and don't be shy about tipping the help."

After I leave Mom and Reed to get settled in, I go to my own room to telephone Alex. The phone barely rings before she answers it.

"They're here," I say. "George is making tea. Come on over."

———

Reed and I excuse ourselves sometime during the second pot of tea. Mom, George, and Alex are so deep in conversation, they barely notice we're leaving.

"So show me this town of yours," Reed says, breathing in the fresh spring afternoon.

"We'll take my car," I say. "It already knows its way around. I'll drive; you relax and sightsee." Once we're buckled in and ready to go, I say, "Where to first?"

"Well, we might as well start with the site you think will work for the distribution centre. If that's not right, nothing else matters. I contacted the regional building authority and land titles office. Though the property isn't currently designated commercial, there are no residences in the area any more, so getting it rezoned might not be a big deal. They sent me a map. There's definitely enough property for the facility and the price is negotiable, so I just need to see how much development it's going to need."

I nod. I don't want to get my hopes up, but what Reed has said so far sounds promising.

We park the car and walk the entire abandoned building site, inside the chain link fence, as well as the field beyond. Reed pulls a pencil and notebook from his jacket, jots some notes, and makes a few sketches. He squats down and scoops some dirt into a plastic bag. I'm dying to know what he makes of the place, but he doesn't say a word. I don't want to jeopardize the outcome, so I swallow back all the questions I have and silently follow behind.

Back at the car, he stuffs his notebook and pencil back into his coat and casually kicks the edge of the pavement. "You're right about the roads," he says. "They would definitely need to be redone if we moved the distribution centre here. Mind you, it looks like they need to be redone anyway."

I'm almost afraid to ask in case Reed's already

decided against the place. "So — would you like me to show you the rest of the town?"

He puts on his sunglasses, so now I can't even read his eyes. "Might as well," he says in a voice that gives me no clue where he stands. "It doesn't look like there's much else to do."

That doesn't sound good. But I can't let myself get discouraged, so I squelch my misgivings, put the car in gear, and morph into a tour guide.

I show him the community hall, emphasizing how it is the hub of Farrow. I take him up and down the winding roads, pointing out how well cared for the homes are. At least the ones that are occupied. Suddenly I start noticing how many houses are empty. It's the same along Main Street. There are a couple of blocks of mostly boarded-up buildings. It's like I'm seeing them for the first time — as Reed must be seeing them. If I'm overwhelmed by the bleak emptiness, and I already love this place, I can only imagine what Reed must be thinking.

In an effort to undo any negative damage my tour may have done, I abandon downtown Farrow for the town's more appealing natural features. I take Reed through the most scenic parts: the fields, the streams, the woods. Finally we end up at the cemetery.

As I turn off the car, Reed glances at me sideways. Even behind his sunglasses, I can tell he's puzzled.

"Come on," I say. "I'd like to show you something."

I lead him to the graves of John and Hannah Swan. "This is the old couple who took Sam in when he was a baby," I say, crouching down to pinch back a couple of wilting blooms from the bouquet between the headstones. I look up at him over my shoulder. "You know the crumbling basements in that abandoned building development I showed you?"

He nods.

"Well, one of those basements was theirs. I don't know which one. But when it was a whole house, Sam lived there."

We're both quiet for a minute, and then Reed asks, "Is that all you've been able to find out?"

I shrug. "More or less. I spoke with one of Sam's foster families. They're the ones who sent me here. And I've spoken with locals who knew the Swans or remembered Sam as a little boy — people like George, but they can't tell me anything more."

"Don't give up," Reed says. "I'm not saying you should stay here — your mother will make both our lives a living hell if you don't come back to Vancouver tomorrow, but you can still keep looking. I know you're probably a little deflated, but you shouldn't be. You've only just begun to search. Hunting down a person's past isn't easy. If it was, don't you think Sam would have already found answers? That doesn't mean it can't be done, though. It can. I bet there are lots of other avenues to explore. If you like, I'll help you."

"Would you, Reed?"

"Absolutely. I'm always up for a good puzzle, especially if it's for somebody I care about. Besides, turnabout is fair play. You helped me find the future home of the brewery's distribution centre, so it only seems right that I return the favour."

I blink. "Are you freaking serious?"

He grins. "Of course I am. I'm more than happy to help you hunt down your family history."

I swat him. "Not about that. I mean, yes, that's great, and thank you, but did you just say you're going to move the distribution centre here?"

He nods.

"To Farrow?"

He nods again. "Don't go throwing a parade just yet, though. It's not going to happen overnight. There's a lot to work out, but I think it's a good spot. So how about we take one more pass down Main Street. I want to imagine those stores all renovated and buzzing with customers."

I smile and sigh. "Me too."

Chapter Eighteen

EVEN THOUGH REED SAYS there's still a lot to do before the distribution centre is a done deal, I'm sure it's going to happen. He wouldn't have said anything to me otherwise. I'm so pumped, there's no way I can keep the news to myself, and as soon as we get back to The Apple Tree, I blurt it out. Mom sends Reed an *Is-this-true* look. His half-smile answer is all the assurance I need.

But that isn't the only good news. While Reed and I were touring Farrow, Mom and Alex drove to the cabin to see Alex's pottery, and judging by the pile of boxes stacked in George's front hall, Mom bought every piece Alex had, and she is gushing about them as much as I am about the distribution centre. That pretty much means Alex has landed herself a fairy godmother. When my mother makes her mind up about something, she's unstoppable, and she's decided that Alex's pottery is — and I quote — "phenomenal," which means Alex is going to have her work cut out for her just keeping up with the demand.

"This calls for a celebration," George announces, popping the cork on what looks like a bottle of homemade wine. "Glasses are in that cupboard on the end, Joanna."

As Mom takes them down, I notice she includes one for me even though I've still got a year to go before I'm legal drinking age. I would never be offered anything alcoholic at home, and I'm not sure why I am now. It's like the first Thanksgiving I was allowed to escape the kiddies' table. Another of life's milestones. I smile. Maybe, in her own way, my mother *is* trying to let me grow up.

We all lift our glasses and Reed says, "To Farrow and the future."

"And new beginnings," Mom adds.

"And good people," George tags on the end.

———

George invites Alex to stay for supper, but Alex begs off, claiming she has to get started on a new batch of pottery.

"This is all so exciting," George declares during dinner. "I haven't been this high since the sixties."

My mother chokes on a carrot, and I pat her on the back. "It's okay. George has a name to live up to.

It's kind of like truth serum. She has to tell it like it is. She can't help herself. You'll get used to it."

George ignores the interruption. "As I was saying, it's all very stimulating, but let me see if I understand the situation properly." She turns to Reed. "You run a brewery in Vancouver?"

Reed nods.

"And you want to set up a distribution facility here in Farrow?"

He nods again.

"We're a bit off the beaten track, aren't we?"

"Yes, but that's part of the appeal," Reed explains. "Certainly the brewery will continue to ship from Vancouver, but we need a distribution centre that's more central as well, so trucks can reach it easily from the rest of Canada and the U.S. A town like Farrow provides an added bonus over a big city like Vancouver in that it allows easy access — at least it will once the roads are rebuilt."

"And this distribution centre of yours is going to make jobs and bring folks back to Farrow?"

"That's the plan. At the moment, Farrow is a bit of a double-edged sword. Because it has pretty much shut down, there's nothing to keep people here, so property is devalued. That's good for me. I can buy the property I need at a reasonable price. Then, if we can wake Farrow up again, the government will restore services, and those low property prices will attract buyers, and before you know it, Farrow will be back on the map. Then watch land values go up."

"And if Arlo can work his magic," I interject, "all the Farrow artists like Alex will form a guild and finally be able to make a living at what they do. And they won't have to take their stuff to other towns either. The bazaar will become a mega-big fair, operating twice a year and pulling in crowds from all over B.C. — maybe even further. And then when the rodeo is back up and running, Farrow will be buzzing even more than it was in its glory days."

Mom, Reed, and George all stop eating and stare at me.

"Oh," I say, as I glance from face to face. "I guess I didn't tell you about that part yet."

————

The next morning, though I'm still excited about all that's happened and all that is going to happen, I'm also a little depressed. It's time to leave Farrow and head back to Vancouver. I love this little town, and I'm sad to say goodbye. The only consolation is that thanks to Reed and the brewery, I know I'll be coming back.

By the time I hit the kitchen, Mom and Reed have finished breakfast and are lingering over a second cup of coffee. Mom glances meaningfully at her watch.

"We said we wanted to get an early start," she says. "It's already nine o'clock."

"That *is* early," I shoot back with a wink. "George says no self-respecting teenager gets out of bed before ten." Mom gets all parental-looking and opens her mouth to put me in my place. "Relax,

Mom. I'm kidding. I'll have some toast and a coffee, and then I'll go pack, which should take about five minutes. It's a matter of shove everything into my suitcase and zip it up."

"And change the bed," Mom says.

I nod. "And change the bed. So make that ten minutes."

"Hogwash," George sputters. "You're paying guests. This is my bed and breakfast, and I'll be the one changing the beds, thank you very much."

Despite George's objection, Mom shoots me a look that says otherwise, so I mentally add bed changing to my to-do list.

As I pour my coffee and put some bread into the toaster, my cellphone rings. I dig it out of my pocket and look at the screen. It's Alex.

"Good morning," I say. "How did it go last night with the pottery?"

"It was good. I stayed up way too late, though, and now I'm a walking bag of dirt. But I didn't want you to leave without saying goodbye. I can sleep later."

"Why don't you come over? George has a big pot of coffee on. I'm just about to pour myself a cup."

"Sounds good. I'm on my way," Alex replies.

I butter my toast, slather it with George's apple butter, and settle in to enjoy my breakfast. But it's a lost cause, with my mother peering at her watch every two minutes and tapping her fingernails on the tabletop the rest of the time. Finally I wolf down the last few bites, grab my coffee, and head back to my room.

That's where I am when Alex arrives. I've changed the bed, so now I just have to pack my stuff. Fortunately, I've kept all my belongings in the bedroom, so I don't have to roam the cottage, collecting everything.

"Need a hand?" Alex asks as I lift my suitcase onto the end of the bed and flip it open.

"No, I'm good," I say. "It's basically just a matter of making sure I don't forget anything."

"Good." Alex sighs and leans against the wall. She takes a sip of her coffee before adding, "I'm pretty much brain dead this morning, so I probably wouldn't be much help anyway."

For the next few minutes, it's quiet. Alex remains propped against the wall, drinking her coffee, and I buzz around the room, rounding up my possessions and cramming them into my suitcase.

Finally I stand back and frown at the small mountain of clothing and toiletries inside my suitcase.

"You really think you're going to get the suitcase closed on all that stuff?" Alex says.

"It should close," I insist. "It did in Vancouver."

"Yeah, but that was when everything was neatly folded and clean. Now it's all just a tangled mess, and it's dirty. Dirt can be really bulky. Take it from someone who works with mud all day." She grins.

I sneer back. "You're so funny. I suppose I could always refold things, but that just seems wrong. Nobody folds dirty laundry."

"Or you could ask George for a plastic bag and stick the overflow into that. Like you say, it's only dirty laundry, and it's not like you have to clear security at the airport. Nobody's going to be poking through your soiled undies."

"Ew!" I screw up my nose. "That's gross. Maybe if I sit on the top of the suitcase, I can squish everything down enough to get the zipper closed." I glance around the room one more time to make sure I haven't forgotten anything. Good thing too, because I spy the framed photo the Sheffields gave me. I wouldn't want to leave that behind. I point to it. "Alex, could you pass me that picture, please?"

"Sure," she says. She sets her coffee mug on the bureau and then reaches across the bed to the night table on the other side. As she stretches forward, a chain with a pendant slides out from the neck of her blouse and dangles in the air. I stare. Even after Alex retrieves the photograph and is upright once more, I can't take my eyes off her necklace.

"Where did you get that?" we blurt simultaneously. I'm pointing to Alex's necklace, and she's shaking the photograph at me.

"My grandparents have this exact same photograph on their living room wall. It even has the same frame. I've seen it a hundred times." She jabs a finger at the teenage girl in the picture. "That's my mom!"

"Your mom?" I repeat stupidly. "That girl is your mother?"

"Yes. Where did you get this?"

I point to the baseball player. "That's Sam. That's my dad."

"What? This is crazy! Where did you get this picture, Dani?"

A million thoughts are spinning through my brain. If they would slow down, I might be able to make sense of them, but they won't and I can't.

"Are Stephanie and Duncan Sheffield your grandparents?"

She nods. "Yes. Did they give this to you?"

It's my turn to nod. Then I reach inside my shirt and pull out the half-heart that mirrors the one Alex is wearing. I hold it out to her.

"And this? It's exactly like yours. I slide my half-heart next to hers. "Where did you get it?"

She takes a minute to compare the two. The hearts fit snugly together.

"My mom gave it to me. My grandma gave it to her. Her mother gave it to her."

"Where did *my* half come from?" I say.

Alex looks confused. "I don't know. I've never seen another half before, and I don't know anything about it. It's just something that's been passed down through my family."

My heart is beating so fast, it's practically tripping over itself. Something important is happening, and it has to do with Sam. That much I'm sure of. I still don't have any answers, but now I have a whole new batch of questions, and I think I know who I need to ask.

"Do you think your grandparents would know?"

Alex shrugs. "Maybe." She pulls out her phone. "Should I ask them?"

I frown. "Not over the phone." I clutch the half-heart around my neck. "If they know more than they've already told me, they're keeping it a secret for some reason. Can we go and speak to them in person? Would they be home?"

"Probably. Do you want to?"

"Yeah, I do." I grab my backpack and car keys. "Let's go. I'll drive."

As we tear out of my room and race for the front door, I holler to my mom and Reed in the kitchen. "Have another cup of coffee. There's something I have to do before we leave."

Chapter Nineteen

JUST LIKE WHEN I VISITED the house before, it is Mr. Sheffield who answers the door.

"Hey, Grandpa." Alex hugs him and kisses his cheek.

"Alex?" He is both surprised and pleased. When he spies me standing behind her, his expression becomes confused. "Dani?" He glances from me to Alex and back again. "You two know each other?"

"We're starting to," Alex says. "Actually, that's why we're here. Can we talk to you and Grandma?"

He still looks puzzled or wary — maybe both — but he invites us in. "Of course, of course. Come in. Alex, take Dani to the sunroom, and I'll get your grandmother."

Unlike the living room with its traditional furnishings and photo-mural walls, the sunroom is a mini tropical paradise. Fitted with floor to ceiling windows on two sides, it is furnished simply with rattan loveseats, large potted plants, and sunshine. A large ceramic plate I recognize as Alex's work is the sole ornament on a large glass coffee table.

"Nice," I say, running my hand around its edge as I make my way to one of the loveseats.

Alex grins and sits down beside me. Almost immediately we are joined by her grandparents. Mrs. Sheffield gives Alex a hug before sitting on the other loveseat with her husband.

"How nice to see you again, Dani," she says. "I had no idea you and Alex knew each other."

"We met in Farrow," I say. "I saw Alex's pottery at the spring bazaar and," I shrug, "things went from there." I don't bother going into details about our rocky beginning.

"It's such a small world, isn't it?" Mrs. Sheffield says. "Here you were just a few days ago, and now you're back with Alex. Six degrees of separation and all that." She smiles, but I can tell from the way she's fidgeting that she's nervous. She looks at her husband and then back at me and asks, "So, did you have any luck finding information about Sam?"

"That's why we've come, Grandma." Alex pulls the half-heart pendant from her shirt. What is the story behind this?"

Mrs. Sheffield frowns. "You know the story as well as I do, Alex. My mother gave that to me, I gave it to your mother, and when you were born, she passed it on to you. I hope you will pass it on to your own child one day."

Alex nods. "That's what I told Dani. But we both think there must be more to it than that."

Mrs. Sheffield cocks her head. "Oh?"

I pull out my half-heart and hold it next to Alex's. "These obviously started as one whole heart," I say. "Do you know why they were cut?"

"Where did you get that?" Mrs. Sheffield's voice is just a whisper, but her eyes burn right through me.

"It was one of the things Sam left me."

Mrs. Sheffield buries her face in her hands and starts to weep. Her husband wraps his arm around her, and she collapses into him.

Alex sends me a concerned glance and mumbles, "Maybe this wasn't a good idea." Then to her grandmother she says, "Grandma, I'm so sorry. We didn't mean to upset you. Dani is just trying to find some answers about her dad. Please don't cry."

Pushing herself upright and taking a deep breath, Mrs. Sheffield composes herself once more. She impatiently wipes her tears away. "Never mind me. I'm fine. It was just a bit of a shock, that's all. I haven't seen the other half of that heart in over forty years." Her husband places a hand on her arm, but she shrugs it off. "I know, Duncan. I promised Kate. And I've kept my word. But it's time for the truth."

"You're sure?" he says.

She nods fiercely. "Yes. It can't hurt Kate or Sam anymore — not my parents either, and Dani deserves to know."

"Who's Kate?" Alex asks.

"My sister," Mrs. Sheffield says. "My twin sister."

"I never knew you had a sister, Grandma," Alex says.

"She was barely eighteen when she died," Mrs. Sheffield replies. "That was a long time ago, many years before you were even born. By the time you came along, memories of her had been buried. There was no reason to tell you about her, but many reasons not to. Your mother doesn't even know."

She licks her lips and smooths her skirt, and I brace myself for the story that is about to come. When I made the decision to search for Sam, I imagined all the different ways I might find the truth, but I never thought about what that truth might be. The fact that it was intentionally kept secret and that it is upsetting for Mrs. Sheffield to talk about makes me nervous. Even so, I need to hear it.

Mrs. Sheffield's gaze finally leaves her skirt and moves to me. "Dani, do you remember when you came here before and were looking at the photo of the young couple in the living room? I told you they were my great-grandparents."

I nod.

"Well, that's where the heart began. It was a wedding gift from my great-grandfather to my great-grandmother. And when they had their first child — my grandmother — the heart went to her. She, of course, gave it to her daughter — my mother. But when my sister and I were born, my mother was faced with a decision. Rather than give the heart to just one of us, she cut it in two; so like most everything else in our lives, we shared it. And when the time came, we both passed on our halves to our children, though until just now, I didn't know Kate had. I always assumed her half of the heart had been lost.

And that's when the penny drops. Kate was Sam's mother — my grandmother. Which means Mrs. Sheffield is my great-aunt. I blink at Alex. She and I are related too. This is my family. The knowledge is so overwhelming, I have to force myself to concentrate on what Mrs. Sheffield is saying.

"My sister and I were very close. We were mirror twins, identical, but opposite. I'm right-handed; Kate was left-handed. We epitomized the twin cliché. We dressed alike. We finished each other's sentences. Sometimes we didn't have to talk at all. We knew when the other was in trouble or hurt. We were connected in a way only twins can understand. We were simultaneously sisters and best friends. In fact, our world was quite perfect.

"And then Kate got pregnant. She was seventeen. I knew almost right away, though I didn't know who the father was. My parents didn't become aware until Kate was nearly five months along. Kate wanted to keep her baby, but the idea was too scandalous for my mother to contemplate. Though it was the seventies already, my mother was pretty old school and didn't buy into the free love movement. As far as she was concerned, nice girls didn't have premarital sex, let alone keep the products of their indiscretions. So she arranged for Kate to spend the rest of her pregnancy in a home for unwed mothers in Calgary, and when the baby was born she was to give it up for adoption. The nuns at the home would take care of the arrangements. My mother concocted a story about Kate staying with an ailing relative to help out, and that's what she told neighbours and friends."

"Why did Kate go along with it?" Alex asks.

Mrs. Sheffield smiles sadly. "As I said, it was a different time. Hard for you girls to understand, I'm sure, but Kate had no choice. She had no money of her own and no place to go. My parents would have disowned her."

Alex's jaw drops. "Their own daughter?"

Mrs. Sheffield shrugs. "Kate and I exchanged letters constantly. We wrote each other practically every day. How I missed her. I could tell from her letters that she was terribly unhappy, and the closer she got to term the more determined she was to keep her baby. So it wasn't a surprise when my parents got a long distance call from one of the nuns, saying Kate had run away.

"Earlier that same day I had received a letter from Kate telling me her plans, so I had to act surprised by the news and then lie through my teeth about knowing anything. At least I had the sense to destroy the letter after I read it, because my mother didn't believe me. When she'd finished ripping my room apart, the place looked like it had been burgled."

Though I never met my grandmother, my heart aches for her. She must have been so scared. "What did the letter say?"

"It said she was planning to leave. She didn't have

much money, but she had enough for bus fare to Merritt. She told me the bus she would be on and asked me to meet her at the depot. She had an idea of where to stay, but it required a car. I had my driver's license by then, so it was just a matter of coming up with an excuse to borrow the family vehicle. As it turned out, my mother asked me to run an errand, which coincided perfectly with the arrival of Kate's bus."

Mrs. Sheffield stops and takes a deep breath.

"You okay?" her husband asks.

She nods. "It's been so long, I thought some of the sting might have gone out of the memory, but," she sighs, "it hasn't. It still hurts." She pats her husband's hand. "But it's okay. I'll be fine."

Alex and I exchange glances. I don't want to cause Mrs. Sheffield grief, but I want — no, I need — to hear the whole story.

"It was so good to see Kate again. For about ten minutes we just hugged one another. Then I drove her to the family cabin in Farrow. That's where she wanted to go. She had money for some groceries, and the place was comfortable enough, so I knew she'd be all right for the time being. The baby was still three weeks away, so we had time to plan. We both hoped that once the baby was born, our mother would swallow her pride and accept the situation.

"I came out as often as I could to bring supplies and keep Kate company, but I couldn't risk raising suspicion at home, so it wasn't as frequent as I would have liked. The baby came early. There was no telephone service at the cabin, and this was long before the time of cellphones, so Kate had no way of letting me know. To make matters worse, it was the May long weekend, and my family had been invited to spend the holiday at a friend's cottage in Kelowna — so Kate couldn't have reached me anyway."

Alex inches forward on the loveseat. "So what happened?"

Mrs. Sheffield shakes her head. "It didn't go well," she says. "Kate had to deliver the baby alone. She lost a lot of blood, and she realized pretty quickly that she was in trouble. She had to get her baby to safety. During her walks around Farrow — she'd tried to stay as invisible as possible, but she'd still managed to get out — she had seen an older couple working in their yard. Kate said they'd seemed so happy, and she wished that she might find that sort of love one day. Anyway, she lingered too long, and the couple saw her. They asked about the baby, of course, and told her how lucky she was, and how they'd always wanted a child, but it had never happened for them. Then they wished her well, and Kate carried on with her walk."

"How do you know this, Mrs. Sheffield?" I ask.

She looks surprised. "I'm the one who found Kate. She told me. That first night after the birth, while she still had the strength, she walked to Hannah and John Swan's house and left her baby on their doorstep. So when I got to the cabin, the baby was already gone. I got Kate into the car and rushed her to the hospital, but she'd lost too much blood. The doctors couldn't save her. And since there was no sign of a baby at the cabin, my parents chose to believe it had died, and Kate had disposed of it. They concocted a public explanation for Kate's death, but once she was buried, they never spoke of her again."

"You never told your parents the truth?" Alex says.

"No. Kate made me promise. She was afraid that our parents would step in and send the baby to an orphanage. She preferred to think she had found her son a good home." Mrs. Sheffield smiles. "And she had. At least for as long as it lasted. Before she died, though, she asked me to keep an eye on her boy, to make sure he was doing all right. So that's what Duncan and I have done. We got married young ourselves, so there was only a couple of years between the birth of Kate's Sam and our Debbie, and when we learned Sam was being sent back to social services, we took him in."

She sits back on the loveseat and her mouth stretches into a determined line. "And that's the story. I'm sorry I didn't tell you before, Dani, but I was keeping a trust."

My vision has blurred, and my throat is tight, so I just nod. It's a lot to take in, and there's still so much more to find out. But there's time for that, and at least now I have solid ground beneath me. Sam and I finally have a past.

Chapter Twenty

IT'S BEEN THREE MONTHS since the last time I visited Farrow, so when Reed invites me to check out progress with the distribution centre, I jump at the chance to go back. I can't believe changes have begun already.

"Woo-hoo!" I exclaim as he swings the BMW into the highway turnoff lane that didn't exist back in March. "Farrow's big-time now. It has it's own turnoff lane and everything. And look at the sign. It's huge! And it's new, and not hand-painted. *Welcome to Farrow: Population (Growing too fast to count)*." I laugh. "That's too funny. And look there, Reed. Another sign announcing the new distribution facility." I shoot him a surprised look. "Is it really going to be operational by next spring? That's less than a year away."

He waves his hand uncertainly. "Give or take. Knowing how there are always delays, I think summer is a safer bet, but we are trying to hype things up so the residents of Farrow have something to look forward to. We've already started interviewing for jobs."

"How many people are you looking to hire?"

"Initially, probably about one hundred and fifty, but that could easily double down the line."

"Seriously? *Whoa*! That's a lot —" but I'm sidetracked as we turn onto the road leading into Farrow, because gone is the narrow, rutted gravel track, replaced by four lanes of pavement. "*Holy cow!* You didn't tell me there are roads already!"

"So far this one leading off the highway is the only one that's finished. The others are still under construction. You'll see as we get into town."

"Have you started building the distribution centre yet?"

"The plans are drawn up and surveying is complete. There are lots of pegs and spray-painted lines. It's just a matter of letting the bulldozers loose, but we want to wait until the roads are finished before we bring in the heavy equipment."

I hug myself. I can't stop grinning. "This is actually happening, Reed. I can't believe it."

"Well, if anyone should believe it, it's you, because you're the one who set the wheels in motion."

I open my mouth with every intention of modestly protesting, but what comes out is far from modest. "Yeah, I guess I sort of did, didn't I?" I grin.

Reed laughs. "You certainly did. Your mother and I are unbelievably proud of you. I'm sure Sam is too. You set out to find your roots — and you did. Then you set out to save Farrow — and you did that too. You are definitely a lady to be reckoned with. Looks like I got two of those for the price of one."

We turn onto Main Street, and to my amazement it looks different too. Oh, sure, there are still a lot of boarded-up storefronts, but now there are a lot more that aren't. New painted exteriors, eye-catching signs, and sparkling windows winking in the sunlight make me catch my breath. Reed has slowed right down, but even so my head is on a swivel as I try to take everything in. One building has gone from wooden siding to a red brick facade. A display card in the window identifies it as the future home of a postal outlet. Across the street is a restaurant, and next to that a sandwich shop. Both are filled with construction workers. The next sign to catch my attention is The Exquisite Artisan. It is a shop featuring work by local artists. Arlo has clearly been getting the guild operational. There's a grocery store and drugstore too — *already*. In the distance, I can see the service station once again has an operational gas pump. It's all so amazing, I am speechless.

Finally Reed pulls up in front of a barnboard storefront and turns off the car. I look at the building. There are several rusty horseshoes hung above the door and assorted bottles, kettles, spurs, harnesses, and other cowboy memorabilia on display in the windows. The printing on the sign has been branded on. I read it. *Sam's Place — Come and sit a spell*. I instantly choke up.

Reed squeezes my neck. "Come on. Let's go inside."

I let myself onto the street and swipe away my tears before Reed can see. He comes around the car, opens the door to the shop, and waves me inside.

And I melt — my bones, my heart, every molecule of me.

The place is amazing. It *could be* Sam's place. This is probably the coziest room I have ever been in. The walls are whitewashed and trimmed with wooden beams. The floors are barnboard, and there's a pot-bellied stove smack in the middle, amid oak and pine tables and chairs and leather easy chairs, rustic loveseats, and even a couple of ottomans. The walls are lined with shelves, and the shelves are filled with books and memorabilia — mostly cowboy and baseball stuff. Western music plays in the background. Only someone who knew Sam could have put this together. I blink back my tears and look up at Reed. "Mom?" I say.

He shrugs. "She might have had something to do with it."

At the back of the space is a bar, the kind you find in saloons, complete with the brass foot rail. A sign overhead says, *Help yourself to a coffee and muffin, a book, and a chair. Donations gratefully accepted. Proceeds help those in need*.

And then, through blurred eyes, I see them — my three amigos — Alex, George, and Arlo. They're standing behind the bar, grinning.

I totally lose it. "Oh, you guys," I blubber, "this is awe ... awesome! *You guys* are awesome. Thank you for this. It's wonderful. Sam would be so happy."

Now I'm crying so hard, the tears are flowing down my face like a river. Reed hugs me, and then Alex, George, and Arlo are hugging me too.

"You're the one who's awesome," Alex says. "You cared enough to try to save Farrow. You believed in it and us, and you found a way to make things happen."

"Like I told you before, Dani," Arlo grins, "the apple doesn't fall far from the tree. You're definitely your father's daughter."

"Hmmph," George mutters, straight-faced. "I suppose she's all right." When everyone pulls back to gawk at her, she shrugs, but her eyes are twinkling. "Well, the girl might have Sam's big heart, but she doesn't have his curls or his piercing black eyes, now does she? And that's the truth, or my name isn't George Washington."

The prequel to *In Search of Sam*
Truths I Learned from Sam

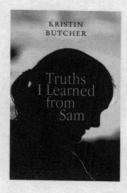

Dani's mother is getting married — again — because that's what she does, and while she and her new husband jet around Europe for six weeks, seventeen-year-old Dani is sent to stay with an uncle she didn't know she had in a small community in Cariboo country she didn't know existed. It promises to be the summer from hell. But Dani's uncle turns out to be an okay guy. In fact, Dani really likes him. And she finds romance, too.

Suddenly, a summer that had doom written all over it turns into one of the best times of Dani's life. Until the bottom falls out. In a story about relationships and about how bad things happen to good people, Dani discovers that sometimes the only villain is life itself.

"The heart of the novel is Dani's relationship with Sam. Butcher handles the pair's growing bond gently and convincingly, while showing compassion and understanding for her teenage protagonist."

— *Quill and Quire*

DUNDURN
www.dundurn.com

Visit us at
Dundurn.com
Definingcanada.ca
@dundurnpress
Facebook.com/dundurnpress